DON'T KNOW MUCH ABOUT INDIANS

(but i wrote a book about us anyways)

Dedicated to Joshua Bear Medicine.

By GYASI ROSS

Cover art by Andrew Morrison. www.onestaa.com
Cover art inspiration by Cheyenne "Shizzam Moe"
Book design by Kim Pyle

Oki. Tsa-nitapi.

Niitaniko Oonikoomsika.

Hi, I'm Gyasi.

Thank you for your purchase.

Now that the formalities are out of the way, let's get something straight. This book is a simple collection of short stories and a few childish poems; it is decidedly not "important." At times, it acts like it addresses some larger and more important issues, but that is a mere mirage, a façade. No, this book is completely fantastical and not scholarly. It does not discuss the essentialization of the Indigenous diaspora It is not a "troubling" and/or "poignant contemplation of the Native American experience." I do not contemplate. I speculate. I throw massive amounts of fecal matter against the wall and hope that some of it sticks. Sometimes it does; a whole bunch of it does not. Make no mistake: this is not a modern day version of our beautiful Blackfeet creation stories, like the ones that my maternal grandpa Percy Bullchild memorialized. I wish it could be considered in that same category, but it cannot. That work required years and years of compiling and research. I did not study for this book. I do not research Indian people. I rarely read about Indian people. In fact, the only "Indian" books that I've read cover-to-cover are *The Sun Came Down, Custer Died for Your Sins, Reservation Blues* and some Ward Churchill book (but that *really* doesn't count as an "Indian" book, does it?). I do not know theories about why Indian people do what Indian people do. I do not pretend to be an expert on Indian people. I do not want to be an expert on Indian people. Heck, sometimes I do not even *like* Indian people. Sometimes I cannot stand Indian people.

>sigh<

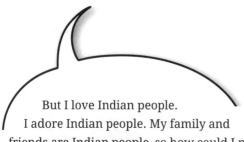

But I love Indian people.
I adore Indian people. My family and
friends are Indian people, so how could I not love Indian people?"
It's only right that I love all things – "me" and "us" – before I love
anything else, right? Therefore, I will always love Indian people. I
have a dysfunctional love affair with Indian people. On one hand, in
my love affair with Indian people, we consistently do bizarre and self-
destructive stuff that breaks my freakin heart into a million pieces.
Then, on the other hand, Indian people (and primarily Indian women)
will mend my heart back up using bungee cords, spit, and electrical
tape and show Indian people's amazing capacity to love and care and
grow and succeed and accomplish whatever we want to accomplish.
I can't stand Indian people. But I love Indian people. I *am* Indian
people. My family *is* Indian people, in all of our flawed and beautiful
promise. Therefore, my intent with this book is to give a few Indian
people something to read. Not very ambitious but very true.

That might not be good enough for some people. I understand that.
Some folks might want more than just some cute stories. I get that.

Moreover, I believe in transparency. I don't want you to waste your
time OR your dime on this if you're looking for something "deeper."
This is not deep. This is shallow. This is 100% based upon observation
and 0% based upon empirical data. If that is "beneath you" or
something that you cannot appreciate, I understand. No offense taken.
I have some "deep" friends – I get it. Sometimes my deep friends and
I simply run out of stuff to talk about because I'm not deep. Also, you
may want to reconsider reading this if you're looking for traditional
stories from a traditional guy who smudges daily and wears
Pendleton jackets everyplace and everyday. I'm not him. The only
Pendleton products that I own are blankets that folks have given me:
my beautiful mom gave me one for graduation, my dear friends from
Rocky Boy Reservation, a few more. I'm Pendleton-less. I'm a seventh
generation mixed-blood Indian, with *very* urban influences, who buys
into the blood quantum dysfunction and plans to enroll all of my
children in federally recognized tribes, just like the rest of my family.
I'm a product of the early-MTV generation who is more likely to have

Dire Straits' *Money for Nothing* or Journey's *Open Arms* in my car CD player than most types of Native music. Except round dance music. I LOVE round dance music. Still, the point remains.

If you're cool with that, well then I think that we can work together and have some fun. These stories are fun, even if sometimes "heavy" and/or "heartbreaking." Indian people are heavy AND heartbreaking. That's who we are – tragic. But we're also magic. We make something out of nothing and turn sad circumstances into amazing success; we are the greatest stew-makers in the world–turning nasty and plain ingredients into comfort food that tastes delicious.

It's all a matter of time. Time is on our side. We are not going anyplace soon; by the way, when I say "we," I mean ALL Natives – enrolled, unenrolled, disenrolled, full-bloods, half-bloods, quarter-bloods; I don't get *too heavily* into the blood quantum/tribal membership politics, so long as 1) your family is recognized as Indian, 2) you wanna learn more about Indian people, and 3) you're not just trying to get a scholarship or a faculty position at a college (FYI: while I lived on the east coast, it seems like people always told me the story about them being white/black/Puerto Rican but with a "little bit of Indian, that's why they have the high cheekbones." I'd reply that I'm just the opposite – "It's funny that you say that because I'm mainly Native, with just a little bit of German and black. That's why I like streudel and fried chicken.")

But I digress. Point is, "we" are not going anyplace – Native people will be here. Promise.

ACKNOWLEDGEMENTS

←——————————————→

I want to thank many people and those people are in my prayers daily. The ones that I want to acknowledge by name are: Likoodzi "Walootsi," Geraldine "Mom," William Ross "Papa," Grandpa Percy, Grandma Maria, Grandpa John, Grandma Rose, Miranda "Geetah-Geetah," Wendy, Neoma, Bobby B.C., Sutah, Manuel "Big Moe," Charles "Lizzle," Tiko, James "Jonesy," David Z., Rion, Big Chuck, Wayne Wanbli, Russell S., Scott W., Scott C., Coach Harney, Alan "Spoon," David/Julian "Comic Book Guy," Willie and Billy F., Hank, Allison and Adacus, Jennifer "Jennifleezy," Arlyn. My "team" Michelle Waits, Amber Hayward, Marci Greenroyd, Matt Hayashi-Echohawk, Andrew Morrison, Kevin Gover, Bill Watterson, Matt Nagle, Kim Pyle and the great City of Seattle. Also, thank you to the Blackfeet Nation, Starr Skoo, Browning, Heart Butte, Babb, Moccasin Flats, etc., the Suquamish Nation, the Puyallup Nation, the Nisqually Nation, all Nations, all tribes, clans (except the Ku Klux, but including the Wu-Tang), bands, pueblos, reserves, First Nations, ANCs, etc.

Please enjoy.

TABLE of CONTENTS

THELMA

They just didn't know how much she hated them. Despised them. Thought about how undeserving they all were. She smiled at them, but it was a smile that would have preferred to put a dagger in their hearts.

Still, she wished that she were them.

Thelma had so much contempt for all of them. She wished that God would point his long, bony, brown finger at them and magically, slowly rip the skin off the pink meat stuck on their bones like a little kid peeling an orange. They weren't worth the hundred thousand or so dead skin cells that fall off their carcasses every day. They were sorry excuses for "adults." She despised them and gave them evil eyes every single time that they stumbled into the house pissy drunk. She furrowed her brow at them and whisper-hollered, *"Don't wake up the kids!!"*

Never mind that it was their house. Didn't matter. The person who rocks the cradle rules the house, or something like that. She would, despite these losers, teach these kids to be responsible, appreciative and loving. She was on a holy mission from God, like the Blues Brothers. She had to be strong to counteract their inadequacies. They were pathetic.

Still, she hated them. Deeply. Yet, despite despising them, Thelma kept on watching their kids.

It was God's plan after all. Since He wanted her to do this – to be the one voice of sanity and strength for these little Indian kids, she would. If He wanted her to let all of these beautiful Indian kids live in her tiny trailer with her, Animal Hoarder-style, she'd do that too. She trusted her God. She loved her God. Completely. She just didn't agree with His decisions; in fact, she hated His decision-making at times.

Thelma was hopping mad at God's judgment. She usually didn't question the wisdom of God. She took things on faith her entire life. She knew that "faith was the substance of things hoped for and the evidence of things not seen." Even when she watched her mother waste away with cirrhosis of the liver, she believed that God had her best interests at heart; she figured that perhaps her mother's death would be the impetus for her father becoming a better dad. He didn't. Still, at the *very least* her mom's death encouraged Thelma to not ever pick up a bottle. In turn, Thelma hopefully will encourage some of these kids not to drink because it destroys Indian people. She could always find a silver lining to these dark clouds – she always trusted God's judgment.

Not here though. She simply did not think that He made a good decision here.

See, God already determined, long ago, that Thelma was unworthy to have children. She was barren. Infertile. Cursed. Worthless as a woman. Especially worthless as an Indian woman. An Indian woman is only judged by her ability to create and maintain families, single or married – not the way white women are judged: the size of the wedding ring, or how long they can ignore their husband's philandering. No, breeding and being the backbone for the family is the *only* criterion to be a great Indian woman. Indian people love to make poems and essays and songs about strong Indian matriarchs – Indian people love their moms. Almost every single Indian man looks back glowingly at the hardships that his typically single mom endured while altruistically, selflessly raising him. She will never be that. She will always be "Auntie Thelma" to kids she's not even related to but she loves. She will never get a Mother's Day card that says "For Mother."

She felt that God made a big mistake by cursing her.

She would take darn near anything that her God had to offer. Anything. Any punishment or test that He gave to Job, she would take it smiling. No problem. Anything. Still, for some reason God took away the "thing" that she wanted more than anything – children. A family. Nurturing her own baby. Breastfeeding. She prayed and prayed for years that God would repeal His punishment; maybe He would, one day, exchange her many, many good deeds for a beautiful, brown Indian child.

Maybe He would take away her sickness. Like He did for Job. Cure her. Be her Balm of Gilead. Touch her with His healing hand and say, "It's ok my good and faithful servant. Be proud of your faithful walk and let your daily mothering serve as an example to your younger Indian sisters. Teach them how to be amazing moms. Show them new techniques of breastfeeding. Your loins are now fertile. Ye are hereby knocked up."

Boom! The Big Bang! Immaculate conception. Science and religion living harmoniously.

CURSE

Thelma thought back to her first sexual encounter. Like most of her friends experimenting with sex at the time – she was 14 – she was stupid, alone, uninformed, and scared. She was also unprotected. Also, like most young Indian girls' sexual interactions on her reservation, her experience was with an older boy. "No, those things hurt me – the latex makes me break out," he told her when she made a meek request that he use a condom. She didn't vocally agree to have sex without a condom, but she let him make his move and didn't fight it. Def Leppard's "Pour Some Sugar on Me" played in the background; it was a hot July day. She was self-conscious about her body. She knew that some boys looked at her and she caught some staring at her developing breasts. Still, she would not take off her shirt. He was older, so they probably were not as big as he wanted. The heat of the day, combined with her leaving her clothes on, and her anxiety caused her to sweat before anything even happened.

He was tall and lanky and handsome. He always wore a baseball cap turned backwards with his light brown braids sticking out. She met him at the Sinclair's gas station where he worked; he smiled at her and flirted with her as she grabbed a piece of pizza.

"Holay! Isn't that your fourth piece today? Gawwwwwwwww..." She shyly smiled back at him. The next day she came in to get some gum and he asked her where she lived. She told him and he said, "Gee, that's only about six houses from me – you don't live there! You've been stalking me! You probably even know that my parents are gone for awhile, down in Great Falls while my dad gets surgery, ennit? Stalker. Don't be stealing any of my movies – I have a lot of good movies, you know. I'll know if some of them are missing."

He winked at her. She blushed and walked away, popping a piece of gum into her mouth.

The next day she stopped by his house. She smiled when he opened the door and she asked him which movies he had. Turns out that he didn't even have a VCR. Heck, the TV didn't even work.

Still, he was charming. She tried to pretend as if he seduced her, that she was a helpless and powerless victim to his male charms and strength. In hindsight, however, she couldn't lie – she wasn't innocent. She wanted it to happen. She felt awkward about her new, developing body; he made her feel pretty. Special.

The experience didn't feel special though. The experience lasted less than three minutes. She knew that it was only three minutes because she knew Def Leppard's "Hysteria" cassette by heart. It was her favorite tape. The boy climbed clumsily on top of her right when "Pour Some Sugar on Me" began and he was done before "Armageddon It" came on. Since "Pour Some Sugar on Me" was only about four and a half minutes long – she hummed to the song while he clumsily pumped away – she knew exactly how long it took. Wasn't it supposed to be longer than this? More enjoyable than this?

Still, that three, maybe three and a half minutes changed the rest of her life. That older boy left her with undiagnosed pelvic inflammatory disease. The disease caused her fallopian tubes to scar, permanently blocking them and virtually eliminating any opportunity for the thing that she wanted more than anything the world – a baby. She wanted to make the baby a cradle board, with beads hanging from the arch so that the baby could coo and play with it, and make her moccasins and teach the little girl, if the baby was indeed a baby girl, how to bead.

But God said that Thelma wasn't worthy because of the bad decision she made. She could never bring herself to listen to Def Leppard again. She hated that boy even though he did nothing wrong. He probably didn't even know what he did to her. She was the one who let stuff happen without insisting on him using a condom. It wasn't his fault. It was hers.

INCONSISTENT

← ——————————————— →

God didn't like her promiscuity. The crazy thing was, it seemed like God thought that *every* other girl over the age of 14 on this cursed reservation was "worthy." Every girl except for Thelma. Even the promiscuous ones. It didn't seem to make any sense. She would sit, watching and seething at different events, thinking "It's *so* incredibly easy for these little girls to have all these beautiful little babies. And then when the baby is first born, like clockwork, everybody gets so excited and coos and kaws at the babies. All the family members brave their way through the snow and wind and whiteouts on the road to get to the hospital to see them. And the first couple of weeks are beautiful times for the baby – mama breastfeeding and looking deeply into the baby's soft and perfect eyes."

But then it always happens – every flippin' time.

That new mother starts to feel not-so-pretty and chubby. Oh, the poor wittle girl. She misses being a pretty, unattached girl. She misses having no responsibility. The new mother has the greatest miracle in the world in her arms, just wanting to be around her all the time. But like clockwork, two months after the baby's birth, the mom squeezes her fat butt into those jeans that *used to* fit and goes to the same tavern or stick game or basketball tournament where she met this baby's dad. She wants attention. She gets tired of the baby getting all the attention. She needs to feel special, dammit, not some little greedy baby!

The little chubby moms knew exactly where to go to find a reliable babysitter. Desperate to get back to their active social life, they'd go over to Thelma's house and pretend that they wanted to talk to her, and make small talk for awhile. Or sometimes those new mothers would come over to Thelma when she was in the grocery store or doing laundry at the Laundromat. No matter which way they approached or where they approached her, and no matter the small talk, those new moms inevitably asked her if she could watch their babies.

The way it always went was this: the mom would talk with Thelma for awhile, and then smile giddily and somehow bring up the topic of a date. She would then look around at the surrounding area and talk quietly as if it was a big secret that she "had a date" (even though nobody really "dated" on the reservation – there were only about four places that a person could conceivably go on a date). Thelma would act excited for her, as if the story of her previous boyfriend – the deadbeat baby's dad who never comes around – didn't start off exactly the same way. Then Thelma, sweet lady that she is, would save the young mom from the awkwardness of asking by saying, "Well, if you ever need anybody to watch your baby, let me know." The young girl's eyes would light up. Then the mom would tell Thelma "thank you" for watching the baby and tell her that she "never gets to go out anymore" and smile mischievously as if she had big plans for the night. Thelma would smile at the young girl and say, "Of course, it's not a problem."

But Thelma didn't mean it when she said it.

It was a problem. In fact, it was a *huge* problem around the reservation. These adrenaline and smile-filled first dates with guys who simply want to get lucky lead to a disproportionate number of Indian kids no one wanted to watch.

As a result, Thelma watched so many unsupervised, unwanted, unloved and unappreciated little Indian toddlers running around in random playgrounds or under the bleachers at pow-wows. Nobody seemed to ever really know who these kids belonged to; they recognized them but didn't know their names. Everybody always saw those little Indian kids at playgrounds – noses snotty and diapers with big nasty loads dripping down onto their little legs – playing normally, as if they were supposed to run around with nasty diapers. Those kids were used to this lack of supervision. They were used to being faceless and nameless – just some dusty rez kids nobody loved or inquired about.

Thelma has already watched generations of those same unsupervised kids. She watched them throughout their early adolescence and followed them into their sexually experimental teenage years, when many of them became parents themselves. She watched them repeat the exact same cycle as their parents (and probably their grandparents as well, although she couldn't say for sure): unsupervised, unwanted, experimental, then parent. She wondered if it would ever stop.

And through it all, God still found her to be the unworthy one. She just didn't get it. Sometimes she would go outside and pray, through tears. She just wanted to understand. She wanted to get it. Why her? There was very little that would make her question God – this was one thing that would. Maybe it wasn't her place to "get it," but she at least deserved an explanation. Didn't she? Why are these terrible parents so much more worthy than her?

RAZORS

The lonely mom asked. Of course, Thelma always smiled and said "yes." Thelma watched these unsupervised kids while their parents went out to party like teenagers. The parents always seemed to think that they still *were* teenagers. Still, she loved watching these beautiful kids.

She also simultaneously resented every moment that she watched these beautiful kids. She resented that the parents did not see the specialness and "gift" that every one of these kids are. She put these unwanted kids to bed at a decent hour while their parents got smashed. She read to the unloved kids. She had to bring her own children's books to many of their houses because the phone book was the only book that she could find there. There never seemed to be a toy to be found either – it was as if the parents intentionally stripped every element of "kid" out of their lives. It was as if as soon as the weekend comes (and many times before the weekend comes), the parents want no more reminders that they have big responsibilities and mouths to feed at home. It seemed like these young parents that she babysat for, much like girls, just wanted to have fun and unfortunately, they simply didn't see the kids as fun. At least not after the fun part of making the kids. It seemed as if their houses were dedicated to *not* acknowledging their children's presence. Since there were no toys around, the kids learned to use non-operable curling irons and old disposable razors as toys.

Ahhhhhh, the razor blades. She always knew exactly what happened when she came to watch the kids and the kids' eyebrows were gone – lack of toys in the house. She saw it a million times; so she started bringing her own toys: Transformers™..., dolls, balls and stuffed animals. So that, for *just one night*, those beautiful little Indian babies could know what it felt like to be desperately wanted and appreciated.

Those kids would feel worthy.

DREAM

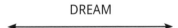

One night after babysitting for an early-20s couple with 5 kids between them, Thelma dreamed fitfully all night long. She dreamed that her God visited her. The strange thing was that in her dream, "her God" looked just like Adam Beach. Also, in her dream, her God (who looked like Adam Beach) also wore fancy ostrich-skinned cowboy boots, like the ones that the short Mexican cowboys wear, and nothing else. He had bedroom eyes. He walked over toward her slowly as she lay on the bed. At first she thought that he was trying to be sexy; she soon saw, however, that his cowboy boots were just new and looked uncomfortable so he couldn't walk like he wanted to. He looked at her dreamily, like movie stars with only ostrich-skinned cowboy boots are wont to do.

"Adam?" Thelma asked. She was a bit intimidated. She was a bit angry. She knew, in her heart of hearts, that this was a dream and that she would simply wake up angry and unfulfilled. Still, she would enjoy it while God/Adam Beach was right here.

"No, Thelma. I am YOUR God. I am the one you always talk to, my good and faithful servant. Hi, babe." God, looking like Adam Beach, smiled at her.

Thelma responded with a smile on her face. "You look a lot different than I thought. Thank God." She always pictured her God as an old man who looked like Old Lodge Skins from "Little Big Man." She knew that God probably didn't look like George Burns, and she was glad because she didn't want to serve a nasty, wrinkly old white man that smoked a lot. Still, Old Lodge Skins wasn't too much better.

This was better. This was a pleasant surprise.

God spoke to her in his best bedroom voice. He didn't have the best voice in the world; it was kinda hollow. Still, Adam was dreamy enough that it sounded amazing and holy and sexual at the same time. "I am here to take away your curse. You have shown yourself to be faithful. You believed in me even when others made fun of you for your belief. You believed in me even before you knew what I looked like. This is kinda a nice surprise, ennit? I've been working out. But you didn't care about that – you served me before you knew that I was a dreamboat. You *are* my favorite servant, Thelma. You are amazing. Your faithfulness will be rewarded. You will give birth to a beautiful baby boy. You will call him Adam."

As Adam uttered the word "rewarded," her alarm went off loudly. She fought it; she wanted to get her dream back. She yelled and cried in her dream, "ADAM!!! I MEAN GOD!!! COME BACK!!!" He did not come back. She woke up with tears in her eyes.

She opened her eyes to face the real world. "Cripes." Thelma had a disgusted look on her face. She wished that she would have simply woken herself up when she realized that she was dreaming. Now, she was sexually aroused, frustrated and still had to go to work. What a stupid dream, she thought. Idiotic. You know that's not real.

Within twenty minutes, Thelma threw up – exactly at 8:30 AM. The next morning, she threw up at 8:30 AM again.

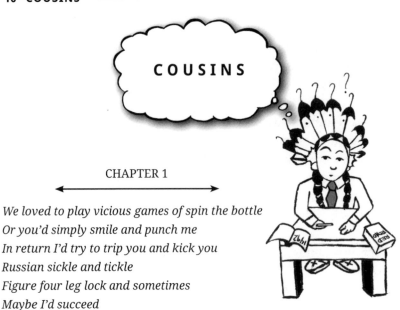

CHAPTER 1

We loved to play vicious games of spin the bottle
Or you'd simply smile and punch me
In return I'd try to trip you and kick you
Russian sickle and tickle
Figure four leg lock and sometimes
Maybe I'd succeed
A little
But
You were so much stronger than me back then
So you'd quickly pin me to the ground
And
Tickle me till I
Cried or peed.

Remember
We used to think that we were first cousins
Heck, we had the same last name and our parents were always together
So we played tetherball and Easter egg hunts

Your mom was my auntie
Your dad was my uncle
He was also big brother, dictator and policeman
Always watching us
Sadly
Remember that time he found us smooching lips
In your pantry
You said, "I'm madly in love with him daddy!"
Grabbed my hands proudly
He got madder and whupped both of us badly

Told us, "Don't you ever touch your cousin like that again."
It took us many years to discover that
We weren't cousins at all
In fact,
We're not even related
Our last names are a horrible coincidence
As babies we kissed a lot,
Therefore,
Our parents told us we were cousins
To keep us separated
But your grandma...your beautiful grandma
She spilled the beans to you one weekend when she was giving you a perm
And you vacated her premises so quickly – hair still in rollers
You were just elated
Ran over to my house, ready to run off to Vegas
Or at least hold hands publicly.
"We're not cousins, cousin – now we can get married!"

We were about 14 then
And that's about the time that your parents sent you off to Chemawa.

CHAPTER 2

←——————————→

You cried the night
Before your long Greyhound bus ride
You sighed, lips swollen from crying, and told me, "We've barely ever kissed.
That time in the pantry doesn't count
Cousin
We were barely even six."
You brushed your tear-soaked salty lips
Over my quivering bottom lip
One hand squeezing my cheeks
The other on my hip
You moved your mouth down my neck
I knew something was amiss
My stomach twisted in knots
Eyes scrunched shut
You promised me that you'd leave me with something to miss:

I got tense – you told me to relax
You breathed inelegantly
On my adam's apple
Said your sister showed her boyfriend that she loved him
Just like this
And it hurt a bit when you did it – you bit my neck
I felt you sucking in my skin
Pulled away,
"Ouch!"
But it was too late to resist
I rubbed the raised skin filled with blood
"Owww"
When you were done.

You told me to look in the mirror
"Oh wow – it's so red. How am I gonna hide this from mom?"
You told me, "You don't hide true love, cousin."
And I won't hide it either –
"Give me one too. Dark red."
I gave you two because I thought I messed up the first time
They looked like the number "8"
We were worn out
Didn't know what was supposed to happen next
We just embraced
You laid your head on my chest and we both fell asleep
It was so late
Later than we ever stayed up together in our lives.
I held my pee all night
I didn't want to stop cuddling.

The next morning when I woke up to go to the bathroom, you were gone.

CHAPTER 3

I wrote you every other day
And you wrote me immediately after
The first letters you sent
Were filled with the scent
Of Aquanet

I could smell your desire to come back home

My letters were filled with butterflies, nervous energy
You tied my stomach in knots
I told all about my first week of class at my new school
But couldn't tell you my happiest thoughts
The doodling on my Science Book
"Me" + "You" = "A lot."
My romantic flights of fancy
Unrealistic fantasies
That are fastened to my brain
You come home for Spring Break
Never go back again
And your daddy doesn't look at our handholding
With complete disdain
And looks of pain.

Your next letters told me all about your new friends
And all the sounds that you would hear
In the middle of the night through your brick dorm walls
How you were scared at night – you cried the whole first two weeks
But then those sounds became normal
They became the sounds of "home."

I sent you a tape to help you to conquer your fear
It was a Maxell 120 minute tape
Everything on it from Maxwell to Tears for Fears
You said, "I played that cassette out, cousin
Thank you so much, dear.
It got me through the night
When the songs played
I could hear you singing loud and clear.
And now
I'm comfortable here."

In fact
You were so comfortable
The school year wasn't enough
At the end of May

You decided to stay.
Get ready for volleyball – we hadn't seen each other in nine months
Phone cards were too expensive
We only spoke once
I felt like I was losing you
Cousin
I was desperate to have my cousin back.

CHAPTER 4

We haven't written in 2 years
I hear you're coming back to the rez
It doesn't sound like you'll be back at Chemewa
From what your daddy says
Senior year will be here
Forrest and Jenny again
I'm glad.
I'm nervous.
I'm mad.
I'm stoked.
We haven't spoke
I feel forgotten
I'm jealous and I ain't going
To your little welcome home party
"Mom, I don't want to go"
10 minutes later I found myself
In the backseat of mom's car
Sulking and pouting when we arrived at your house

The door was open
It was May and sunny
You poked your head out the door and smiled at me
I couldn't help but smile too
I tried to hide it
I smiled larger
Put my chin down to conceal my zeal
Didn't realize I'd be this excited
Can't believe this moment's real
You're finally home.

We're finally together.
We're finally old enough
To talk about forever
Without someone saying
"They're just young
They don't know any better."
Finally
Unabashedly
Without fear of your father bashing
My skull
I can show you how happy I am
To see you
I flash the cheesiest most sincere smile I own
You step fully into the doorway
I step to meet you in an embrace
Happy to see me too
Said, "Thank you so much for coming to my place."
I saw your figure
Belly protruding
You must have seen the confused look on my face
"Nobody told you, Cousin?
This is my baby shower."

WILLOWS

The little boy sat crying. He tried to fight the tears; he was a tough 8-year-old boy, trying very hard to show his mom how much of a "tough guy" he was. Still, his face betrayed his attempts at tough guy-hood; his face was red, his chest was puffed out, as if that's what a tough guy did. His chin was up. His bottom lip stuck out and trembled as he attempted to keep his voice from breaking.

He was mad at his mom. Pouting. But he didn't want to show that he was pouting because he wanted her to see him as an adult, capable of making his own decisions. She didn't see that.

"Jason, I really do not care if you cry. You're going to wear it, boy. I don't care if you get teased – sometimes teasing happens."

His mom is a beautiful and young Indian woman by the name of Patricia. She tried to reason with him, but Jason was barely 8 years old and getting teased was the absolute worst scenario that could happen to him right now. Really, it was the worst thing that could happen to almost any kid at that age. Kids are just cruel, and at 8 years old he was just starting to understand social standing and that some kids are "cool" and some kids are "not cool." Like most kids, he wanted to be cool; it seemed to make life easier. Still, his mom didn't seem to care. "You'll get a lot more than teased if you take it off – you *do not* disrespect your uncles."

Jason knew what that meant. He knew it meant that there were going to be no more negotiations. He'd heard it a million times before – his "uncles." Some uncles; it was so cruel.

He thought about the few times he got into *serious* trouble with his mom. She would make him take the long walk to the brush about a quarter of a mile from his house, down by the river. When he got down to the brush, his mission was to look for the skinniest and wettest little willow branch he could find. His mom called these branches "a willow." These little skinny branches didn't look imposing at first glance – in fact, they might've even looked slightly dainty. Then, Jason had to take out his little pocketknife that he won playing "The Claw" at a pow-wow. He loved that knife (he snuck the knife to school a lot, just so that he could feel tougher). Next, he'd peel the willow just as his mom taught him to do – scrape off the skin pointing the knife away from him so that he would not cut himself. Underneath the willow's skin, the meat was fresh and cool. Wet. He then brought the wet, fresh and cool willow to his mom so that she could let his uncles do their business. The uncles' business was correcting him, and they did that business well.

It took a long time for Jason to collect these willows. It gave him a lot of time to think. The long and drawn-out process really gave him way too much of an opportunity to get scared and realize how pointless it was for him to get into trouble.

His mom's voice brought him back to their current conversation. Her voice got softer. "Look, Jason – I love you more than anything in the world. I know that there are going to be things that *seem* cool at first. I'm not going to lie to you and tell you that those things aren't fun. But many of those things are going to hurt you in the long run. There's *always* going to be stupid friends around you who will try to get you to do the wrong thing, Jason. They will make it seem fun. It might even *be* fun while you do it. But I promise you that *you* will be the one getting in trouble for it. They will not. The sad fact is that their parents don't care for you like I care for you – they let them get away with anything that they want. I won't do that. I'll keep you from doing stupid stuff, one way or another. Your uncles will keep you in line. Just like now. I don't want to, but I will call your uncles."

She reached her hands toward his face, using her fingertips to wipe his tears downward over his cheeks. Sure, she was in tough, single mother mode – that certainly was never going to change. Still, she was also a loving mother, one who loved her baby boy more than anything in the world. That instinct made her want to comfort her baby right now. Jason pushed her comforting hand away from his face gently and turned his head away from her hand.

"I'm not crying, mom. You don't have to wipe my eyes," he said, snorting his snot back into his nose, "I'm not a baby, mom. I know I'm supposed to listen to you. But...I don't want to wear it anymore." He tearfully tugged at "it" – the object of his consternation that he desperately wanted to take off.

"It" was a necklace, made of a dried, brown and skinny willow limb; it was a piece of a tree called the "autumn willow" that grew wild in this area. He wore it around his neck twenty-four hours a day, seven days a week since as long as could remember. The "necklace" did not look particularly unattractive; it also was really not that noticeable at first glance. But it was one of those things where, if someone *did* take the time to look for things to tease about, it stood out. Jason pled and pled that he was, in fact, the only kid at his school who had to wear a tree branch around his neck. He oftentimes tearfully told his mom, "...I don't understand why you like torturing me!"

It was fair to say that he wasn't happy about the skinny willow necklace that his mother forced him to wear. After all, kids are kinda cruel. Kids who go to poor schools – such as Jason's school on the reservation – seem to be even crueler. It was as if these reservation kids, since they were deprived of so many things financially and materially that they really only saw on television, sought out kids who were even more deprived to make themselves feel *somehow* wealthier or more like those kids on television.

Pointing out differences wasn't unique to Indians or to reservation kids or to poor people. It just seemed like there was a bit more of a willingness to do it there. But the cruelty was similar to many other elementary schools.

Like most elementary schools, all of the kids in his class liked to point out pretty much anything "different" about any kid in class; it didn't matter if the different thing was thick glasses, a cleft palate, torn clothes. All of those things (and many more!!) were all fair game. For example, Jason remembers the time one of his friends wore wristbands that were really the cut-off, colored stripes from tube socks. As nice as Jason was, even *he* was cruel to his own friend. It really was hilarious – did he *really* think that kids were going to think that those were "real" wristbands? Still, the teasing never really got out of hand because *everybody* wanted wrist bands – he just wanted them slightly more than most people.

But the necklace was a completely different animal altogether.

The necklace represented an even easier target for cruel kids, because it was something that no one understood. Sadly, everyone – even in 3rd grade – knew where cleft palates came from. Everyone knew where bad vision and the desire for cool wristbands came from. But nobody understood the branch necklace – they just thought he was some weirdo kid who couldn't afford a real necklace. The kids made up their own stories about the necklace – they teased him and said that Jason's dad was a tree, and that this was the only thing that his dad left as a reminder.

Jason knew the truth – his dad wasn't a tree. That was stupid. Still, that didn't make it any easier to wear that stupid necklace around. "Well," he thought, "I guess *part* of it is true: daddy *isn't* around and never really was." Jason knew – even though his mom tried to never talk rugged about his dad – that he got scared off when Patricia was pregnant with him. He also knew that he stopped coming around about three weeks after Jason was born; he brought diapers, formula and some fingernail clippers for Jason during those first three weeks. Evidently he tried to be a "good dad" for a little bit. Still, that was the only "child support" that Jason's mom ever received from him.

Jason also knew he had a half-brother that he's never met. Jason learned that fact randomly one day. Patricia and Jason stood in the checkout in the Great Falls Wal-Mart. Another lady standing in the line mentioned that Jason looked like her son. She called her son over from the baseball card section and put the boys side-by-side and lo and behold – they really did look alike. The moms began conversing and deduced that the boys were born within 8 months of each other and lived one reservation apart. Evidently, the boys' dad performed exactly the same disappearing act on the other reservation as well (and the other boy's mom whispered that there were several others that she heard about) – the David Copperfield of reproduction.

The cycle went like this: impregnate, then disappear during the pregnancy. Come back a few days after birth with a nice story about firefighting and/or getting himself right. Buy diapers, formula, fingernail clippers. Then, like Kaiser Soze, he was gone. And it was exactly the same for both boys – now, neither one of these boys knew their dad at all.

But that's not the reason that he wore the strange willow necklace. At least not directly.

Several times, his mom told him the story of why he wore it. It went something like this:

Patricia took Jason to meet his paternal grandparents immediately after Jason's dad left them. She wanted to hate his whole "other side" family, but she could not. She could not punish the rest of the family for their son being a spineless sperm donor. They probably disliked him too. Unfortunately, as she well knew, you cannot choose your family.

That day, as she prepared to make the drive to Jason's grandparents' house, the sun shone brightly and it looked very warm. The sun was misleading, however. The temperature in Patricia's car read 36 degrees. She bundled Jason up extra thick when she came back inside from warming up the car. Her head was full of thoughts. She knew that it was the "right thing" to bring her boy to meet his grandparents; she also knew that her beautiful little boy would need as many role models as possible growing up. Moreover, she knew that it was unfair to make the grandma pay for her deadbeat son's lack of testicular fortitude. She loaded Jason into his carseat, all wrapped up like a beautiful little burrito that only God could cook up, and drove off toward the south part of the reservation. Patricia liked to listen to classic rock and so the car radio was already tuned to the classic rock station:

♫ ♪
More days to come
New places to go
I've got to leave
It's time for a show

Here I am, rocked you like a hurricane
Here I am, rocked you like a hurricane
♫ ♪ ♫

A few hair rock songs later and Patricia and baby Jason pulled up to Jason's grandmother's doublewide right outside of town. The grandma looked out the blinds and happily motioned for them to come in. The grandma was young – maybe only 15 years older than Patricia, and she was still very beautiful. Even though the grandma was young, she definitely had an older demeanor. She'd become an old lady before her time. The two ladies, grandma and mom, had a good visit together. Grandma made incredible macaroni soup and bannock, had a great sense of humor, and Jason took to her immediately.

She swaddled him tighter than Patricia felt it was safe to do but she wasn't going to correct his grandmother the first time that she met her. Patricia instead held her breath while she was wrapping him. Jason responded by falling asleep within three minutes with a contented smile on his thin lips. His grandmother laid him on the couch all wrapped up.

When Jason went to sleep, his grandmother made a pot of peppermint tea and poured a cup for her and Patricia. She told Patricia that she had something that she had to talk to her about. She whispered to her: "A secret." As soon as she handed Patricia her cup of tea and then sat down to join her, her body language changed completely. Suddenly, Jason's grandma did not look like the super-grandma she was just a few minutes ago, making incredible bannock bread and giving "Ancient Indian Secret" baby-swaddling lessons. No, now her body language was meek and sad; she would not look Patricia in the eye. Instead, she looked down at the baby and the couch and floor. Apologetic. Maybe even a little bit "lost."

"My girl," the grandma started, looking down at her cup of peppermint tea, "promise...when you raise that precious little boy of yours...." She kept getting a bit choked up. When she did, she took a swig of tea to clear her throat, "...your boy is incredible. He's beautiful. Please do not make the same mistake that I did when my boy – Jason's daddy – was a little boy."

Now she was on a bit of roll, able to talk a little better. Fresh peppermint tea has a way of doing that. "See, my girl, when my beautiful little boy was first born – my handsome little man who eventually grew up to get you pregnant and make me beautiful grandchildren, but who is a deadbeat, awful dad – I told myself that I was going to be a tough parent. I told myself that he was going to be the first high school graduate in our family. Heck, I was gonna make him go to college! I knew that I owed it to him to hold him to high standards and to expect the world out of him. Just like you with Jason, when I first saw him, I fell in love. I knew that love was tender but also tough, and I also knew that I did not want him to be like the other kids on the rez, drinking and carrying on. So I was always behind him. Constantly. I was always on his case."

She took a deep breath. "But then his dad walked out on us when he was two. And even though I tried very hard to be a great wife, I felt guilty about his dad leaving. I felt like it was my fault somehow. Even though I knew that there wasn't a darn thing that I coulda done about him leaving me and my son. I mean, I desperately wanted him to stay, but I still felt guilty. I knew that my boy was suffering inside, because his dad was gone, even though he looked happy and playful on the outside. I didn't want my boy to suffer, so I promised myself that I wouldn't ever let him suffer again if I could help it."

The grandma's shoulders hunched as if this was a great weight to tell Patricia this. The baby lay there still, smiling in his sleep, with little traces of milk on the sides of his mouth.

The grandma continued her confession, Catholic-style. "The truth is he wasn't suffering. He was a little kid. Little kids adapt to change much easier than adults do. *I* was the one in pain and fearful of loss. So I kept him way too close, because I didn't want to lose his dad *and him*. He became my security blanket, my obsession."

"As a result," Jason's grandma continued, "I turned my boy into a spoiled brat. I let him get away with anything. Whenever he got into trouble, I got mad at the people who got mad at him. I never got mad at him or stopped to think 'maybe there's a reason that *everybody* seems to think that he's rotten.' But no, I crafted conspiracy theories in my mind: 'everybody's out to get my boy.' If his grades were bad in school, it was because the teacher did not like him. If some other parent kicked him out of their house, I said that the parent was just jealous that their kid was not like my boy. I lied and told the attendance office that his absences should be excused. I'd always say that he was sick or that I was sick and he was taking care of me. He never took care of me – I have no clue where he was when he was skipping school. But I did that. I made him into the monster that he is today. I still love him, but he's a monster. And the 100% dead honest truth, my girl, is that I created that monster. Nobody else."

Jason's grandma's eyes teared up when she said that. It was as if she had a realization when she said the words, "I created that monster." It was as if she realized that for the first time. She took a sip of tea very slowly, to catch her breath and her composure.

"I realize now, my girl, that I wasn't loving him all that time. Every time that I protected him from facing consequences, I wasn't loving him. He needed to realize that consequences are a crucial part of everyday life. That's not love. That's hate. That's idolatry. That's setting him up for failure. Loving him would have been spanking him hard *each and every* time he lied to me or hollered at me or skipped school or smoked weed. But instead I made excuses for his bad behavior – I shielded him from God and everybody else who woulda punished him. I told myself that it was his dad's fault that he was like he was. The truth was that *he* made those bad decisions, not his dad.

Every single one of us has hardships – I see it now, *you* have a hardship being a single mom. Still, you have to do it. You have no choice. You can't wake up one morning and say, 'I don't want to live with the consequence of my choice to have unprotected sex with a loser.' Life doesn't work like that. And now, I have to live with my decisions to be a bad mom back then – and I tell you, right now, I'm sorry my girl. I'm apologizing to you, woman-to-woman, mother-to-mother. If only I had spanked him, he wouldn't be so ignorant. But I raised him to be a mama's boy, a sissy. I raised him to depend on me each and every time he got into trouble. I wanted him to depend on me! I *wanted* him to need me so that he wouldn't leave me like his dad did."

The young grandma looked down at Jason on the couch and started to sob loudly. Patricia reached over Jason, wrapped up and looking like a glow worm, and started rubbing his grandma's hair. Patricia said, "It's ok. You didn't know what you were doing at the time. We all make mistakes – I don't blame you. Honestly."

Jason's grandma looked up and wiped away her tears with her forearm and wrist. "I know you don't, my girl. What's done is done – unfortunately, I can't do anything about that now. But around here," the grandma paused, "history repeats itself. All the time. I don't want it to repeat itself with Jason, my girl. You're his mom and you are in control – I understand that. But I'm asking you, *begging* you to make a promise to me. I can't make you promise me, but I'm asking you to."

Patricia wanted to comfort her. She'd suffered a lot. She could tell that she was sincere – she didn't want to control Patricia as a mother. She wanted to help her. So she responded in the only way that she could. "Of course. I know that you want the best for Jason. What do you want?"

The grandma's eyes were very serious. She stopped looking down. She was happy that Patricia was at least interested in what she had to say. She looked directly in Patricia's eyes. "I want you to promise that you will not make that same mistake that I did with Jason's dad. I see so many parents on this reservation raising their kids in exactly the same way I raised my boy. Their dads are not around and so these little boys run around being little smarties, talking back to their moms. Their moms don't do anything about it because they're either too tired or they feel guilty about their men leaving.

"This reservation is going to be overrun by those smarty little boys pretty soon because those moms simply will not do anything to stop those rotten little boys' disrespectful behavior. If they understood what that does to their little boys the way that I understand it, they would do something about it. But they don't and those beautiful-yet-rotten little boys are going to grow up soon. It happens so fast, my girl. And when they grow up, hopefully a few of them turn out okay; but most of them are going to be terrible men. They're going to be criminals and dopeheads and deadbeat dads like my son. Patty, you cannot do that to my grandson. I want you to be quick to whip him with a willow when he does bad, and be quick to praise him when he does good. Most importantly, I want you to teach him to know, love and respect his uncles. The uncles are for more than just spankings. They're for teachings."

The grandma's request took Patricia aback a little bit. She didn't mind spanking. She was spanked, and her parents were pretty good about never being abusive and always staying consistent. Still, she didn't see it as a cure-all and didn't really understand why it was such a big deal. The grandma saw the hesitation in her face and responded without Patricia needing to ask the question.

"It really is that important, my girl. I wouldn't ask you to promise otherwise. Our people have a story about why the Creator put those willows all over this area. They say that the willows were always good friends to our people – those willows let us use them for a million different purposes back then. Now, they call these particular ones 'Pacific Willows.' Anyway, these willows promised to be good friends and protect us as long as our people spent quality time with them. When we did that, they would work to keep our household together and safe. And they upheld their end of the bargain. Always. For example, they were our first ropes and they were always strong enough to tie things together when we needed. Also, they allowed us to ground up their bark into flour. They protected us because we could use the stems as our bows and carve their ends sharp into arrows; when someone tried to move aggressively against our camp, those willows made sure that we were alright. And finally, their beautiful, flexible, skinny branches..." the grandma's eyes lit up when she discussed their branches. "Their branches were like the perfect uncles that were always around. Once they hit us kids' backsides, we listened like perfect little angels."

She continued, "Our people were great friends with the willows. We were always together – using the willows to help hold together our structures like dance arbors, shelters and ceremonial structures. And the willows were great uncles. The only thing is, like all 'best friends,' they wanted to spend time with us. And since we moved to this 'modern society,' we don't use willows for houses, any other type of construction or even for spankings anymore. Now we have cinder blocks and two by fours and tent poles for our structures. Since we don't 'need' them anymore, or so we think, we don't really spend that much time with them anymore.

"Progress happens, and thank God that we have these modern structures and modern things like 'time out' for kids. Those new things are good and Indian people have always been resourceful and willing to embrace technology. But just because there are new things doesn't mean that we abandon the old. That's a very white way of thinking. We adopted that way of thinking when we abandoned our uncles, those willows. And that's one of the main reasons that Indian people have so many problems now."

She was upset. By this point, Patricia couldn't really tell whether she was more upset about her disappointment as a parent or by the lack of interaction with the willows. Or both. Either way, the grandma could barely get her words out without crying. "Promise me, my girl – promise me that you won't make the same mistake with Jason that I did. Please let Jason spend time with the willows and let them be his uncles and friends. Not just for spankings – people think that old people just want to spank kids all the time. That's not true. They're for teaching. He needs to learn how to make bows and ropes and flour and his own structures, tree houses and tents, with those willows. I wish I had made my son study with his uncles. I think he'd be a completely different person now."

Patricia was stunned at her honesty. It must have been so painful and so difficult to admit that she "messed up" raising her son. Of course Patricia knew that she'd made mistakes raising Jason;

sometimes she felt like she made more mistakes than successes as a parent. Still, every parent wants to believe that they usually made the right decisions, but Jason's grandma was under no such illusion. And she spoke so openly, in such an honest and humble and painful way – it wasn't a "small" admission of fault. Instead, she admitted to the ultimate failure as a parent, confessing that she sent her son on the path of being a deadbeat dad.

All of it sank in for Patricia. She did not want to feel the same pain that this unfortunate woman did. She also did not want Jason to not know what accountability was. Most importantly, however, he was growing up in a rough place. People lived rough lives here. Patricia wasn't sure that she believed wholeheartedly in the whole "uncle" aspect of the willows and about the supernatural relationship that existed between her people and the willows. Still, she knew that Jason needed any head start that he could find in this rough place. Therefore, if the willows gave him any level of instruction and helped him to be successful and navigate his way through the early part of his life, she was thankful. Coming from this rugged place, what did she have to lose? Things were rough here; she had an obligation to take advantage of everything that might help her little boy get ahead.

"Of course I will. You're right. Thank you so much for telling me this story. I promise that I will not let Jason be a spoiled brat. I will make him have the relationship with the willows that our people have always had. You've done good – you might have struggled as a mom, but you're an incredible grandma. You're amazing. Thank you for telling me this. I give you my word right now. Matter of fact..." Patricia touched the sleeping baby gently on his head and got up from the couch. She opened the front door to the grandma's trailer. The grandma lifted up the blinds on the window and watched Patricia as she went outside and walked down the rickety stairs and toward the brush about a quarter of a mile away. The grandma sat down with Jason and rubbed his forehead gently and sang Cyndi Lauper's "Time After Time" to him.

About 15 minutes later, Patricia came back into the doublewide smiling. She held up a very skinny, very young willow branch with little buds on it. She began to pull back the skin on the branch slowly, almost painfully, like peeling off a scab. She used her fingernails to make sure that the whole willow was peeled clean and exposed the whitish-green raw flesh underneath. The willow, it was barely thicker than a shoestring and about 12 inches long. She lifted her burrito-wrapped baby up under the upper part of his back and supported his head on her forearm. She then bent the willow in half and tied the skinniest end around and in a loop into a knot. She then doubled the knot several times and wrapped it around his neck.

"Grandma, I promise that I will bring him up close to the willows. He will wear a necklace made of one of his uncles every day as long as he is in my care. I will make him a new necklace every single summer when the willows are new and we will spend time with them making stuff and weaving things out of their limbs. Jason will constantly be around his uncles, whether that means making a bow or whipping his butt with them. Either way, he will know that his uncles see what he does and they care about him and will do something if he acts in a way that they do not like. He will not be like his dad. He will wear this willow on his neck or his butt – and I will let the willows and the spirits and the grandfather take care of him as long as he lives in my house."

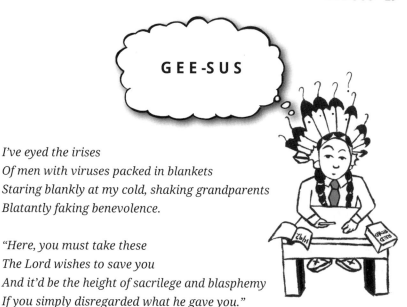

I've eyed the irises
Of men with viruses packed in blankets
Staring blankly at my cold, shaking grandparents
Blatantly faking benevolence.

"Here, you must take these
The Lord wishes to save you
And it'd be the height of sacrilege and blasphemy
If you simply disregarded what he gave you."

My grandpa grabbed the blankets
Suspiciously
But it was freezing cold this particular season
And although they had heard stories-myths
About white killers
They had no particular reason
To doubt these religious men
Dressed in black
Who talked about
"GEE-sus"   "GEE-sus".
My grandpa told me that since these men have these warm blankets in this frigid cold
This "GEE-sus" must be good.

My eyes have seen the result of this decision
To accept these gifted blankets that these men offered as a symbol of their religion
Days later chills, a rash and a fever that obscured my grandma's vision
And when my grandpa started to vomit he to told me to leave the village
"Run as fast as you can
Don't hesitate or wait
There's a spirit in these blankets

Evil in the wool
All our people who have touched them..."
He trailed off
Eyes full of blood
Steam rising from his head
I turned around to run...

This "GEE-sus" musta got him

I ran to the next village
Wool blankets over dead flesh
Frozen red blood out of their eyes
Steaming vomit still fresh
And I'm freezing
But can't touch the blankets
Because "GEE-sus" is still upset
With my people
Therefore I must ignore the wet
Biting, freezing cold on my feet
Pretend the bitter wind does not exist
Find a fire somewhere
Because maybe the fire can resist
"GEE-sus'" blankets.

But I don't find a fire
Only more blankets on cold flesh
And I'm so cold
So I have to grab one
These woolen messengers of death
That seem to have killed all the Natives
Because it's so cold
So I pull it closer to my chest
And it feels so good for a moment
I fall asleep
Watching my breath.

Bernadette woke up on the morning of Tuesday, the 21st. "Ech," she muttered. She had a horrible taste in her mouth. She knew better than to drink that coffee late last night. The clock read "6:43." She could've gone back to sleep for another 17 minutes and still made it to work on time easily, but she didn't fight to go back to sleep. Why would she? It was pointless; 17 minutes wasn't going to help her. She needed 17 more hours of sleep. Heck, 17 days of sleep would've felt nice. But since she could not have those 17 hours or 17 days of sleep, she figured she'd get up and face the brutal day. She propped herself up on her elbows and told herself very quietly, "Today is the first day of the rest of my life. I'm gonna get up even though I don't want to." She stretched her eyes open, wrinkling her forehead. "I *have* to make today different."

Bernadette sat up. She looked around and took a deep breath. "Be thankful," she reminded herself. "Find something to be thankful for." She scanned her body as if she were literally looking for something to be thankful for at that moment. She couldn't, however, think of anything. All she could think of was what was wrong: she was hungry. She had cottonmouth. More than anything, she just felt painfully, excruciatingly *tired*. She felt as if she were dropped into a wild river from a boat and forced to swim against the river's fierce current, spitting out water and struggling to breathe in order to stay alive. She literally could feel herself drowning in life's vicious currents, tired and trying to get herself to a safe rest spot. The harder she swam, the more she seemed to float downstream. She desperately needed to plop ungracefully down on the rocky, uncomfortable river shore and melt into the ground.

Tired.

"This reservation is getting to me. All these ignorant people." She closed her eyes briefly and shook her head. She tried to ignore all the negative images – the stuff that she typically focused on – and think of something for which to be grateful.

Still, as Bernadette sat up and kicked her legs over the side of her bed, she had to face an uncomfortable fact – she was not Superwoman. She was not her mom or her aunties or her grandma. She simply was not the romanticized, strong-hearted, long-suffering Indian matriarch who could put the world on her shoulders, make bannock bread, and still put on the "good face" with perfect skin without ever breaking a sweat. All the women in her family seemed to do that – no problem. She could not. That realization was a shock to Bernadette's system. She actually got tired. That was almost illegal in her family; it seemed like her mother never, ever got tired.

As she stood up to get out of bed, she thought about all the amazing women in her family. It seemed like her aunties and grandma never got tired – they were always taking care of someone or something. Not Bernadette though. At this moment, she was profoundly exhausted. As she turned the bathroom light on and looked in the mirror over the sink, she could see how tired she was: her eyes drooping, bags under them. She wished that nobody expected anything of her. All she wanted to do was – as if she *really did* wash up on that river shore – eat something, drink some water and fall back asleep in the fetal position.

She looked at herself in the mirror and murmured to her reflection, "You, young lady, are a failure as an Indian woman. You are supposed to never get rest and be happy about it. You are supposed to make wild and disgusting love to your so-called man all night and then wake up and be extra sexy in the morning." She heaved a deep sigh and turned on the cold water. She cupped her hands and splashed the water over her face. It gave her a slight headache but it felt so good. She looked back up at the mirror and tried to smile. She failed miserably. "But all you want to do is listen to Delilah at Night and go to sleep for six days."

She hated this rez. She hated the people on this rez; it seemed like the people were only in her life to cause misery. It didn't seem any of the people in her life – *especially* friends and family – ever had anything good to say about anybody. They were ignorant. Still, she had to be honest, "ignorant people," much like her job, kids, boyfriend, bills, etc., have always been here. It just seems that it's only now that she's begun to allow those ignorant people to steal her joy and her energy. For some reason *now* she's given them room to make her miserable.

She used to do a pretty good impersonation of her mom, aunties and grandma; like them, she never let those ignorant people get her tired in her life. Until recently. Now, they live under her skin.

And she wasn't only physically tired now. She was tired of her life. She was tired of the crap that filled life every day. She was tired of people who insisted on filling the days with crap instead of beauty. People like her boyfriend. People like her sisters. She was just tired of "negative people" – she simply didn't want any more negativity in her life.

She looked at herself in the mirror and began to talk to herself again. She tried not to chuckle – it was so ridiculous to have a "serious" conversation looking at herself in the mirror, she thought. Still, as ridiculous as she felt, she had to do this. She furrowed her brow and spoke in her deepest, most serious tone, "I'm going to make a promise to you, Bernie. I know you're tired. I can see it. You look terrible. I know you feel terrible. So I'm going to promise you that I'm going to make changes that will make things better for you and me. The *first* change that I promise you I'm going to make is that I'm going to change the way I interact with negative people. I'm not going to let them ruin my days or steal my sunshine. Misery loves company. They will not have my company – I will not allow them into my house to gossip."

She was getting more comfortable with having serious conversations with herself in the mirror. "Bernie, today is the first day and the most important day. One day at a time, just like those triple A people, Bernie. The Creator gave you this day to change your life for the better." She finished her speech to herself, "That is my singular goal and promise to you for today, Bernie. I will change how I interact with negative people and negativity. If you die tomorrow and you did not change this small thing, you will not have accomplished your purpose, Bernie."

She turned the shower on and fought to keep her eyelids open. Sure, she was tired, but she was going to win this fight. She was going to get the things that exhausted her unnecessarily out of her life. Her plan for the first day of the rest of her life: she would make a list of the things, situations and people that she needed to either get *out* of her life or at least dramatically reduce the amount of influence that they held *within* her life. "I've got to make a list. I need to tell myself the things that I am tired of and that I will no longer stand for. If I don't stand for something, I'll fall for anything. I've been a fool. I've been falling for anything." She walked into the bedroom of her one bedroom trailer to take a look at the clock while the water warmed up – the clock now read "7:01." She had to be at work in 59 minutes.

The shower felt amazing. She talked to herself intensely throughout the shower. She coached herself through the bathing; it felt as if she were literally washing her previous life off of her. She felt, as she scrubbed hard with her loofah pad and actually scraped off the surface of the skin on her shins and forearms, that she was exfoliating the drama, fatigue, manipulation and ignorance off of her. She felt like a new person.

She got out of the shower and peeked her head out the bathroom door to look at the clock. It read 7:47. "Wow. I took a 45-minute shower?" She was going to be late. She looked into the steamed up mirror and wiped an area clear. "So what?" she said to herself. "I need to get my plan together. If I don't stand for something, I'll fall for anything. I have to do this."

"This is much more important," she sighed as she left the bathroom and walked toward a nightstand near her bed. She fiddled around in the drawer but could not find what she was looking for. Then she looked down on the floor and noticed a piece of folded up paper. She reached down to grab it; it was her court notice for a DUI a few weeks before. "Stupid. I know better than that. Now I have to go to court and I know I probably won't have to go to jail but this was stupid and it's going to cost me an arm and a leg." She opened it up and read it briefly. "Wow. I blew a .16. I was really blitzed that night. That's the first thing I have to change – I'm going to write my list on the back of this DUI – my reminder not to let myself ever be so stupid again."

She sat back down on her bed and turned the court notice over and began to write:

CHANGES TO THINGS THAT BERNADETTE SIMMONS IS TIRED OF
– EFFECTIVE IMMEDIATELY – EXPIRES NEVER
THINGS THAT I'M TIRED OF THAT I'M GOING TO CHANGE NOW:

1) *Pretending that my boyfriend loves me even though he lives 10 minutes away and I see him once a week.*
2) *Pretending that to my boyfriend, it's more than a relationship of convenience.*
3) *Pretending that there are "no good Indian men out there."*
4) *Pretending that the real problem is that I'm too lazy and/or impatient to find a "good Indian man."*
5) *Pretending that I'm helping my kids by getting upset at someone every time they criticize them.*
6) *Pretending that my kids do not need criticizing.*
7) *Pretending that I don't notice when my kids come into the trailer drunk.*
8) *Pretending that my kids' ADHD or ADD is the reason that they won't listen to me or anybody else.*
9) *Pretending that I don't notice how so many people are on pills nowadays and seem to be simply trying to stay awake all day, at the job and elsewhere.*
10) *Pretending that this pattern of Indian person attacking Indian person is "normal" and "that's just how life is."*
11) *Pretending that there is nothing that I can do about Indian person attacking Indian person.*
12) *Pretending that I cannot speak up when I hear someone running down another Indian person when I'm around.*
13) *Pretending that I cannot stop those people from running other Indian people down in my office or my house.*
14) *Pretending that us being poor is "normal" and using where I live as an excuse to always be poor.*

15) *Pretending that I'm doing my best as a parent and that my kids' behavior is nobody else's business.*

16) *Pretending that the bad behavior of my neighbor's kids – the ones who keep breaking my windows – is NOT my business.*

17) *Pretending that all of us parents are not responsible – by not being strict with our kids – for the increased crime and drug use on this reservation.*

More to come. I'm gonna change this; I'm not gonna be tired again.

Signed,

Bernadette

She went to work late that morning. She didn't get there until about 11:40 am. Her co-workers looked at her from the corner of their eyes, smirking. She didn't make any excuses for her tardiness. She just went about her business, smiling. She was tired, but she found something for which to be grateful. She took a stand. Her standards were right there in her pocket in writing. She wasn't going to fall short of them again. Nobody was going to make her swallow her standards again.

That made her feel strong, despite her tiredness. Her co-workers looked at her and wondered why she looked so happy. She usually looked so tired and "beat." Defeated. Her co-workers took solace in the fact that she always looked so glum. She looked wonderful today; she glowed with power and confidence.

She didn't engage in any gossip during lunch. She knew that would probably mean that all of the gossip would be about her. She was fine with that.

Bernadette made three copies of her letter about half an hour before she was scheduled to leave work. She giggled because she was using work's resources to make her life better. She chuckled because she knew that most of the time it seemed like work just made people unhealthy. This time she was using work to change her life around and make herself much healthier. She liked that.

Right before she left work she hung up one copy of the letter at her desk. She took one of the copies to tape on her bathroom mirror. Finally, she resolved that she would laminate a copy and carry it with her at all times. She could feel that this was the beginning of a new life.

Bernadette smiled as she walked out to her job's parking lot. It was brisk out. The cool air woke her up. She thought to herself, "The 21st will be better than the 20th. The 22nd will be better than the 21st. You are the luckiest woman on the planet because your best days are all ahead of you."

He was 22.

He met her when she was 14
Courting doesn't happen here.
They were more inclined to watch movies in the
basement
Of his mother's house
He introduced her to beer
Long before he introduced her to his dear mother
And that only happened because his 5-year-old brother
Happened to overhear
Eavesdropping
In the basement Lil Brother heard gruntings and groans
Mike sat up quickly
Prevented climax
Thinking they had been alone
His mom came downstairs and told him
That if he gets this little girl pregnant he cannot raise the baby in her
house.

Mike could see the hurt in his mom's eyes,
With one look he knew
It wasn't so much the baby that threatened her,
It was this "little girl" that threw
Her shirt on so embarrassed, put her eyes down out of mom's view.
Mom knew that Mike had been with girls before, but this was her baby and
she could sense something new
Mike was in love. Or at least he thought he was.
And the only woman that Mike was supposed to think that he loved was
his mom.

Now his girl is 17, and pregnant.

They swore they'd be together forever.
Now they've been together for 3 years
Living together and playing house
Mom came by from time to time
And gave dirty looks to the girl.
She made hot tea and cleaned up the
One bedroom apartment no furniture.

On Sundays
Michael and his sweetie pie drove into town to explore the stores
Several guys would try hard to look into her eyes
She'd make sure to lower her face and look at the floor
But her beauty was beyond what her shyness could disguise
They adored the five foot four brown skin indigenous features she wore
Tantalized
They fantasized about being on her side
Not a day more than 17 but very mature
Mike raised his chin high and said "Hi" to the guy as they passed by
But then Mike would call her "whore" when they walked in their apart-
ment door
Chastise her venomously the moment they stepped inside
She tried to reassure him until she couldn't take it anymore
And she ran off into the night.

But of course she always came back.
Especially when she got pregnant – she was old fashioned
Every baby needs its father.

She was remarkable
Still he was careful never to remark or speak
About her beauty or her grace
Her sunny presence and disposition
Which was the essence
Of radiance and benevolence
Gave him good loving plus cooked for him every day.
He felt unworthy.
Old.
Nasty.
Filthy.
Dirty.

Gollum in possession of his precious
Hands do not deserve the sacred object that it touches
Still
Since God somehow put Beauty in the Beast's grasp
He must hold it forever.
No one can have it
Lest he carve out their eyes
Spit in their sockets
Wanted her soul trapped in a locket forever on his chest
A heart shaped box to keep the rest of her
Bound forever
Wished that he could eat her cancer when she turned black.
She would surely leave him to start a family
With some handsome guy who deserved her more than him
Slim trim, well-hung good looking with braids as long as his limbs
Mike was none of those.
His prospects were grim
Dimmer than the night that was quickly approaching.

"I need to keep her.
No one can have my precious."

He picked a fight this Sunday night
"I saw you smile at James."
She ignored his comment
She knew that he was just ringy
She started putting away the groceries
He wouldn't let her
Grabbed her arm at the wrist
He wanted a response
He had four cans in the car
And four more since he got home
And the alcohol in his blood
Made the demons start swinging at him
Spit in his face
Call him a pussy
His face scrunched up
Turned bright red from the insult
Warrior instinct came out
"You can't talk to me like that!"

She was sweet
Tried to calm him
Stood by where he sat
Said "Mike, I'm not your enemy –
I don't want to fight."
She put her hand on his head to soothe him.
Tipped his head against her slightly swollen belly.
"That's your daughter in there.
Be nice to her."

He bit the hand that comforted him
Spit at the life-giving Goddess in front of him
That sought to love him regardless of conditions
Still
Jealousy put him in a godless condition
He knew that she would leave him
Needed her to justify his love.
Insecure.
His Madonna
His lucky star
Came to him just like a prayer
Asked him to be a father figure
To her
Their baby.
He committed blasphemy
Sacrilege
He knew she held eternal life in her womb
And the maternal hand on his cheek
Plus her soft voice and cheap, sweet perfume
Almost stopped him
From being Pontius
His voice broke for one tenth of a second
His drunken courage momentarily went away
But he faked his way through trepidation
Ready to begin the brutal ballet

He had to destroy something beautiful

"Don't you ever touch me like that

Bitch
You speak to me like I'm a kid
Nothing you say will make it better
I saw loud and clear what you did!
You smiled at James
You were never mine
I was never yours
I bet that baby isn't mine!"

He was crying – he got up, turned and walked away
She walked behind him, sobbing
Grabbed his shoulder gently
He jumped slightly
Turned around
Grabbed her arms tightly
Put thumbprints into her light brown skin.

"I told you do not touch me!"
He threw her by the shoulders down to the linoleum
She whimpered
Tears mixed with Vanilla Fields
Fetal position
Like the miracle in her belly.

He took another drink while standing over her
Finished his ninth can
Tried to spit on her but instead puke ran down his chin
"How dare you sleep with another man?"
He was crying
So was she
She still tried to grab his hand
Legs wobbly
Pulled him off balance
Michael could no longer stand
Fell on his old lady
Knee landed on her head
Mike passed out on the kitchen floor in his own vomit
Next to his queen
She lay there dead.

TRAUMA

(Part 1 of 4)

| ☐ PROF. RICHARD HED | ☐ >> Re: "FINAL PAPER" |

"About freakin' time. Sheesh."

Michael First Rider was excited to see the email in his Gmail© inbox. It was now exactly one week after his Native Studies class officially ended, and this was the last grade that he was scheduled to receive. Now he was done! The rest of his grades were very good. He wanted to hurry up and get on with his summer break – he planned to take a trip to California to see some relatives that he just met online on Facebook; apparently his uncle married some rich Indian lady down in Southern California about 30 years ago and they had a gaggle of kids. They were wealthy, so they were going to take him to Disneyland and Seaworld and a bunch of other places that Indians don't go to; he was super-excited. Still, he couldn't go *anyplace* until he knew that school was a done deal.

Now that Professor Hed (finally!) sent him his grade, school was officially a "done deal."

Michael wasn't crazy about Professor Hed. Yeah, Hed was a very prominent Indian academic and Michael knew that he was kind of a big deal and that white people thought that he was God's gift to Indian people. What those white people didn't know (or didn't care) was that, like most Indians that white people like, no Indians would ever know who Professor Hed was if he walked into a pow-wow or a round dance. Still, Professor Hed wrote books and that was remarkable for Native professors. He was rarely in class because he was always out lecturing to some white people about why Natives do the things that they do.

It was kinda sad – Michael thought that he found a "mentor" type with Professor Hed and was excited to work with him; still, he quickly realized that he had little in common with Hed. Hed didn't come from an Indian community and had spent very little time among Natives. In fact, the one "Indian" trait that Hed *did* possess was that he was chronically late – Indian time must be nature and not nurture – and it annoyed the living heck out of Michael. "Figures," Michael thought. "The one Indian teacher in this entire school and he's the one who cannot seem to get his grades in on time."

He clicked the mouse to open the email and was surprised to see how short the message was:

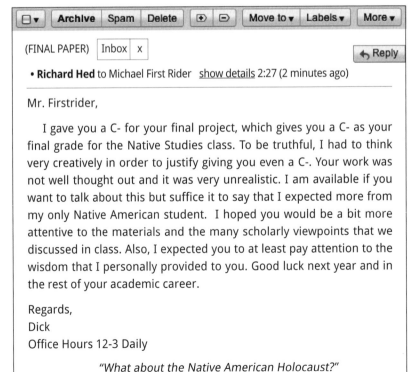

☐▾	Archive	Spam	Delete	⊕	⊟	Move to ▾	Labels ▾	More ▾

(FINAL PAPER) | Inbox | x   ↩ Reply

• **Richard Hed** to Michael First Rider   show details 2:27 (2 minutes ago)

Mr. Firstrider,

I gave you a C- for your final project, which gives you a C- as your final grade for the Native Studies class. To be truthful, I had to think very creatively in order to justify giving you even a C-. Your work was not well thought out and it was very unrealistic. I am available if you want to talk about this but suffice it to say that I expected more from my only Native American student. I hoped you would be a bit more attentive to the materials and the many scholarly viewpoints that we discussed in class. Also, I expected you to at least pay attention to the wisdom that I personally provided to you. Good luck next year and in the rest of your academic career.

Regards,
Dick
Office Hours 12-3 Daily

"What about the Native American Holocaust?"
R.R. Hed

Michael leaned back in his chair and stretched and yawned. That was his response when he was deeply upset – he yawned. He briefly flashed back to his "upsetting times" as a kid, when he used to get into fights. During every single confrontation, Michael remembered, he'd yawn and stretch uncontrollably, meanwhile the other kid always seemed to punch him repeatedly in the jaw. He thought that the kids got even angrier when they fought him because of his yawning – that he was belittling their toughness and acting "bored." He wasn't bored; he was angry. People just showed anger in different ways.

He snapped back to his current frustration – his eyes opened wide and watered, yawning, and he felt just as helpless and useless now as he did during those beatings.

Obviously his grade disappointed him. He worked hard on his project and honestly believed that he took it more seriously than everyone else in the class. He did tons of research, incorporated personal experiences, and gave serious critical thought to his topic. He couldn't say for a fact, but he estimated that he must have put in 80 hours on this project with research, editing and writing. After all that work, to get a "C-" was ridiculous. "That's the grade that they give to people who are stupid and do really crappy work, but because those stupid people work really hard and the professor doesn't want to discourage them, he gives them a passing grade," Michael thought.

"That's not me. I know very well that I'm not brilliant. But I'm pretty smart. At the very least, I'm not stupid. And more importantly, I worked hard. I know that I presented some outside-the-box ideas, but we're in school, dammit! That's what I'm supposed to do. I have to meet with this guy and see what the heck he was thinking."

He typed out an email:

Send	Save Now	Discard	
From:	Michael First Rider <iridefirst@gmail.com>		
To:	Dick.hed@mfu.edu		
	Add Cc | Add Bcc		
Subject:	Expectations		
	Attach a file		

B *I* U 𝒇· 𝑻𝑻· T͟͟ₐ T̲ ✎ ⊕ ☰ ☰ ☲ ☳ **"** ☰ ☰ ☰ 𝑇 « Plain Text   Check Spelling ▾

Professor Hed,

    With all due respect, I think you're wrong about me and my project. First of all, I appreciated and studied your opinions. All of your opinions. I just don't agree with them. At all. I didn't think that was a crime. From the very first article that you had us read, "Why Indians Should Never be Accountable for Anything. Ever." – written by you, of course – I respectfully disagreed with your perspective. I do not think that my disagreement with you should be a basis for a bad grade. It especially should not be the basis for a bad grade when I substantiated everything that I wrote in my final report. You disagree with my views, fine. Still, that should not be grounds for a bad grade. That's just like my disagreement with your views should not be grounds for me to say that your class sucked. I want to meet with you ASAP to see if we can come to a resolution on this.

    I will stop by your office during your regular office hours tomorrow at 2:15.

Thanks,
Mike

        "Self-determination means that we should expect to
have to do it ourselves, stupid."

The next day Michael arrived at Professor Hed's office at 2:15, as promised. He glanced in the large window that provided a "fishbowl"-type view into the Professor's office; he could see the Professor looking at the computer screen, probably checking emails or on Pandora. He walked past the window to the door and didn't knock – the door was open. Instead, Michael motioned like he was going to knock with his right hand, and waved to Professor Hed with his left hand that was holding a three-ring binder. The binder had a simple title page in the front. The title page read:

THE INTERGENERATIONAL TRAUMA TRAP:
Crucial Reasons that Native Americans Must Move Past
Excuses for Poor Performance

A Case Study
By
Michael First Rider

Master of Arts Student, NATIVE AMERICAN STUDIES

Hed motioned through the open door, "Come on in." Michael stepped inside and sat down on a wooden chair. The Professor sat in a plush leather chair and crossed his legs in a somewhat effeminate manner; he opened up a manila envelope and shuffled a few papers.

Michael looked around – the room was full of Native-themed artifacts and articles. The Professor's bookshelf was full of leather bound books, and also held a small family shrine, of sorts, with a half dozen pictures of the Professor and his blonde-haired wife/girlfriend/ significant other engaged in various outside activities – spelunking, hang gliding, hiking. In one, the two of them were literally riding camels with turbans on their heads and with Aquafina bottles in their hands; Michael tried really hard not to laugh at that picture. The lady was a pretty blonde. Several of the photos showed off her extensive turquoise jewelry collection. Michael guessed that she probably had some distant Native ancestry that she liked to mention frequently.

Michael looked over at the Professor – Hed was looking at some notes, presumably about Michael's report. Michael then noticed that directly above the pictures were two very elegant looking paintings. One painting showed Goyathlay looking fearsome, and the other painting was of Quanah Parker.

The awkward silence made Michael nervous. Michael decided to break the silence and yawned his way through his overly gracious opening salvo to the Professor, "Thanks for meeting me on such short notice."

"Of course," the Professor began abruptly, as if he'd been waiting for Michael to acknowledge him out loud before he could begin. "Let me get right down to business, Mr. First Rider. As a starting point, I disagreed with the substance of your email. I do not think your analogy – that your disagreeing with me is equivalent to my disagreeing with you – is appropriate, Michael. The things that I offered you during the class are factual – and you chose to disregard those facts, which is obviously your prerogative. However, we need to be clear that your opinion, if that is indeed your opinion, that the class "sucked," is merely an opinion. Of course you're entitled to have any opinion that you wish, but the right to have it does not make it an objective fact. The things that I said in class and the things that I write about in my books are accepted as fact; they are peer-reviewed and put up to substantial scrutiny. I have no problem presenting them as fact."

"Now, you question the concept of 'intergenerational trauma,'" he continued. "However, Native peoples' inability to perform and excel as a result of historical trauma is proven, empirically, and thus should be accepted as conventional wisdom. I think that shows that there is something inherently *worse* in Native people's historical trauma than in any other ethnic group's trauma; statistics back me up on that. Your paper disagreed with this position – passionately. Personally I, as a Native American, think that your tendency to say that Native peoples' trauma is no worse that anybody else's trauma is extremely offensive and puts you in the position of 'blaming the victim.' It shows that you do not respect Native people."

End Part 1

T R A U M A
(Part 2 of 4)

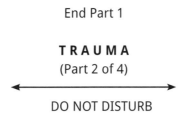

DO NOT DISTURB

Michael thought about what it must have looked like from the big window looking into the office. Professor Hed's door was closed during regular office hours – that was very strange. Unusual. Really, it never happened. Like most professors, nobody ever really wanted to visit Hed, except those few, exceptional kiss-asses who saw these professors-who-publish as some weird celebrity figures. Most people did not, so Hed could have kept the door open 24 hours a day with nobody bothering him. He was famously boring and condescending and infamously narcissistic; he always wanted to talk about whichever book he most recently finished. Even stranger than his door being closed, however, was the *End of the Trail* "Do Not Disturb" sign that indicated that someone had actually visited him at one time, and moreover, the conversation was *perhaps* interesting enough that it required privacy.

Couldn't have been.

It was an odd sight to be sure. A spectacle. Mike tried not to grin thinking about what other students must have thought passing by Professor Hed's office. "Collect your composure, Mike. Focus. Don't smile – he'll know that you're laughing at him," Michael thought. "Listen to what he's saying...he loves it when he thinks that you're listening to him. He probably masturbates to his own audio-books."

He almost broke into a laugh. "Okay, serious face," he thought to himself.

Mike got into his serious face and focused in time to hear the end of Professor Hed's mini-soliloquy. The sad part was that the Professor didn't even notice that Michael hadn't even been pretending to pay attention; he just kept on talking, "Blah, blah blah...something about questioning whether historical trauma is a fact...blah, blah blah... to say that Native peoples' trauma is no worse that anybody else's trauma is extremely offensive and puts you in the position of 'blaming the victim.'"

"Of COURSE Native people's trauma is worse," Hed continued, "even if there are similarities between two different ethnicities' experiences. Even if those two ethnicities appear identical on the surface, they are different and if one of those groups is Native Americans, Native Americans had it worse. See, there are very specific and consistent reasons why Native people have historically struggled worse than any other racial group in the United States. If you would have read and internalized my writings, you would know that the major reason is intergenerational trauma. That is, Native Americans are simply so profoundly affected by historical injustices that it is simply unfair to expect Native Americans to excel. Therefore, it is not fair to imply that it is Native American peoples' fault when they perform poorly in school or perform poorly in professional or family life. Moreover, Mr. First Rider, it *will continue* to be unfair to expect Native Americans to do well in school, professional life or family life in the near future.

"Your paper says that you expect Native Americans to be on equal standing with other ethnic groups – that's just not realistic. Your paper shows that you do not respect Native people. Your paper shows, as I advised you earlier, that you're blaming the victim."

Professor Hed reiterated his point, as if he needed to translate for Michael. "You simply cannot realistically expect Native Americans, in general, to do as well as other ethnic groups because of the trauma that they've faced."

Mike didn't need a translator. At this point, however, he did need to breathe deeply to keep his cool. The Professor reclined back in his chair as if he'd proved his point. Mike, however, figured that the conversation would probably move in this direction and anticipated this exact discussion. He knew exactly where the Professor was going and parried the Professor's point.

"Well, Professor, as a preliminary matter, I never doubted the theory of intergenerational trauma. I'm not sure where you got that from and I seriously doubt that you can point to me saying that it wasn't real anywhere. My paper acknowledged that intergenerational trauma was real. I won't focus on that, however, because that had nothing to do with the overall point of my paper – my point is that intergenerational trauma *while indeed* real, is not unique to Natives. In fact, every single culture and ethnicity suffers from intergenerational trauma. Every single one! What is also true is that, even though every single culture and ethnicity suffers from intergenerational trauma, somehow, intergenerational trauma's *effects* manifest themselves in a stronger and more pronounced way for Natives. That's empirical, and I can accept that.

"But that doesn't stop the inquiry. So I narrowed down the sample size and asked a very specific and very historically provable question. The question that I asked is very appropriate. Why do termination-era Native families show stronger effects from this trauma than Holocaust-era Jews, even though the experiences were very similar and with Jews oftentimes suffering worse traumas? That's not blaming the victim – that's analysis and asking a very fair question. It seems like it's a question, however, that you're uncomfortable with because it undermines the theories in your books, and also because of your..." Michael paused and put his two forefingers and middle fingers into the air to form "air quotes," "...conventional wisdom."

"So tell me, Professor Hed, exactly why is it unfair to ask why

Holocaust-era Jews are doing better than termination-era Natives? It seems like as clear an analogy as you can find. I think I have a suspicion: it goes against your conventional wisdom that Indians cannot be anything other than victims."

Michael took a deep breath and spit out those words – "conventional wisdom" – with particular distaste, as if they actually tasted horrible coming out of his mouth. Mike reclined in his chair, almost mocking the Professor's body language. Professor Hed looked at Michael as if he wanted to respond but then smirked slightly at Michael and motioned for him to continue.

So Mike continued.

"Professor, you say 'conventional wisdom' as if that's supposed to give me or you or anybody else comfort. You act as if 'conventional wisdom' magically makes something 'right.' I see the exact opposite. I see 'conventional wisdom' as religion – 'we're too lazy to see if this is right or wrong, so we'll let this thought go unchallenged.' That seems like the biggest travesty in academia. Yet, that's exactly why you gave me an undeserved low grade; because I challenged your 'conventional wisdom.'

"You did not like the fact that I said that Natives *should* be compared to Jews and all of Jewish peoples' amazing accomplishments because it goes against the theories in your books. I said that we should be compared because our experiences match up; tell me how our experiences *do not* match up. More importantly, however, we should be compared because I know that we *can* compete with Jews and anybody else – we don't need for people to make excuses for us. Still, the only way that we will compete is if we treat ourselves like adults and say that we're responsible for our own actions. Therefore, we must see how badly our professional and academic achievements compare with a group of people with almost identical experiences. 'Conventional wisdom' says that we cannot compete with Jews or anybody else, so we shouldn't compare numbers. It's unfair to the poor Indians. I call BS. I am a 'poor Indian.' I've seen the strength of my people when we're put to the test. We can compete with anybody. Let's see the numbers so we can improve."

An awkward silence followed. Mike wanted to say something to fill it, but his mouth was dry from talking. Plus, he already ended one awkward silence today; he was not going to continue to be the conciliatory one. His cottonmouth allowed him to hold his cool and he looked directly at the Professor. No smile. No scowl. No frown. No blinking. Michael simply looked at the Professor challengingly and unafraid, waiting for a response.

The Professor blinked, but was able to play it off cool because at that very moment, his computer received an email.

That allowed the Professor to still have his dignity when he broke his eye contact with Michael. He looked at his computer, and then down at his desk, as if he were looking at his phone or for something near his phone. The Professor swallowed loudly, and kept the silence going. He felt like he took Mike's best shot – a strong one, no doubt – but took it and knew the answers to the questions that Michael asked. Now, the Professor thought, he could dismantle this young cub at his leisure.

This was Wild Kingdom to the Professor, when some young buck challenged him. He liked this; this actually got Hed's blood flowing.

"Well, that's certainly an entertaining thought. Exciting even. Wow – I'm exhilarated, Mike." Professor Hed refused to look at Michael. He didn't talk for another 30 seconds, at least; he just looked leisurely over his desk, looking for something that apparently wasn't there. Then after an extended silence, Hed spoke in a very low and slow, "sing-songy" tone, as if he were the only one in the office and he were talking to himself. "Comparisons are good for Natives. Native trauma is no worse than anybody else's. Natives can compete with anybody in the world." Professor Hed paused, finally turning dramatically to look at Michael. "Tell me, Michael – I understand that you have *some* small amount of research to support your argument. I get that, that you feel really good and puffed-up that you have some research. I mean, everyone has a website nowadays. Everybody's an expert. Still, you want to get down to the nuts and bolts of your bad grade? Ok, Michael. Let's start with your sources; your sources just weren't credible. Plus, as you so eloquently pointed out a few minutes ago, the notion that

Indians can compete in any marketplace *clearly* goes against almost 100 years of conventional wisdom. I'm a conventional guy."

The Professor looked around, as if someone else might be inside the office eavesdropping on them or listening through the large window. "I'm very conventional; I guess that's why I like conventional wisdom. I like straightforward, Michael. I like my sex missionary; I'm not a freak. I guess you're unconventional, aren't you Michael? You're a bit of a freak." Then he said, dead-eyeing Mike over the top of his glasses, as if he were talking to a little kid, "But I don't really care about your sex life, Mikey. What I really want you to tell me, Mikey, is what it is that makes you such an expert on Indian people? What makes you think, Mikey," as the Professor motioned his hand, like Vanna White showing off a new Ford Focus, toward his bookcase with a dozen books that he authored, "that you know more about Indian people that I do? If you somehow slipped past me and all of my research, I can accept that, but you probably *should* let me know what makes you an expert on Natives? Please, please tell me how I missed this development. Please. I'm all ears."

End Part 2

TRAUMA
(Part 3 of 4)

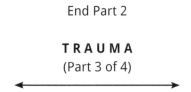

Mike stared at the Professor with his mouth agape. The Professor's last statement – to show him *how* he's more of an "expert" on Indian people – brought back a million thoughts on how men never grow up. "Did Professor Hed *really* just challenge me to an 'Indian-off,' Zoolander-style??" Michael thought, "I guess I shoulda wore my headdress and breechcloth in here. Damn, I thought that I left the insecure game of 'Let Me See How I Can Out-Native the Native' behind in undergraduate. Sheesh." It seemed like *all* the Native kids played that game in undergraduate, attempting to prove through dyed black hair, tanning, war stories, speech patterns and name-dropping, exactly how "Native" they were. Now the Professor, feeling like Michael challenged his Indian-ness, recoiled and put his peacock feathers on full display.

"Collect your composure," Michael thought. "Don't play this game."

Michael leaned back again in his chair and slowed his speech down considerably. He smirked slightly; he was kinda impressed that he got this big-time academic to come down from his ivory tower and show his insecurities. Now Michael was going to play the bigger man. "I really have no interest in showing you that I'm an 'expert' on Indian people, Professor. I'm not at all. That's you, I guess. That's not me. I'm a student – I don't pretend that I have all the answers – that's why I'm supposed to be learning from you. But I *do* have a few ideas, based upon experience mind you, which probably shouldn't be discounted. Now, I know you're into your books," Michael made the same sweeping Vanna White-ish motion toward Professor Hed's collection of books; a collection which consisted mainly of books Professor Hed had authored. There were also other books on a shelf in the **Native Studies** section which someone had neatly labeled with a label-maker. Mike continued, "I know that you read all about us Indian people and I'm sure you've read plenty about the woes and difficulties of the reservation. I'm also sure that you have plenty of big ideas of how and why bad things occur on the reservation to those Indians on the reservat--."

Professor Hed interrupted, "Mr. First Rider, you know very well that I *am* a Native American. Please do not imply that I am not. I am an enrolled member of a federally recognized Indian tribe, therefore a Native American. My father was in the military, so we were not raised around the reservation and I have never lived on a reservation. But that is not the test for whether one is Native American. I am Native American."

Michael stared at him dully. "Right. Yes. I know you are legally an Indian. You told us several times during the class. You said that you made friends with some Native students while you were at Dartmouth, and you know that your family had Native ancestry as well. So you wanted to learn more about your 'roots' and so you started your academic career and interest in Native studies. Yeah, you told me that story several times, Professor. And I told you, I'm not trying to discredit your theories or your Indian sense of identity. I believe that you wholeheartedly *believe* that you're Indian and also that your theories on Indians are based upon some very reliable sources. Cool. Bully for you, Professor."

The Professor nodded his head in agreement, and mouthed "of course" to Mike's concession that Hed's theories were based upon "reliable sources."

Mike continued, "All I know is what I've seen, heard, smelled, touched and tasted. Nothing less, nothing more, Professor. And I've seen – with my own eyes – ," Mike murmured a bit, his eyes narrowing, thinking about the families that he visited as part of the research for his paper. The first family he visited, he met them during the summertime in their dilapidated HUD house; there were at least 12 fly papers hanging from the ceiling, yet seemingly a million flies still flew around the house. The family's name was "LaFountaine," but they didn't pronounce it with the French "LaFontane." Instead, the family pronounced it exactly as it looked, American-style.

Grandma LaFountaine was only 38 years old; her first name was "Dottie" and hated it when her grandchildren called her "grandma." She had her oldest child, a baby boy named Silas, when she was 15 years old. Three more children followed within the next three years, all daughters; the oldest daughter died in a car accident when she was sitting in the bed of Dottie's El Camino on the way to the river to swim and fell out on her head. The children's father died years ago and really wasn't involved with any of the kids anyway. Therefore, Dottie raised all of her children on welfare, and seemed to be habitually in and out of physically abusive relationships. The youngest two daughters, Owena and Thomasina, saw their mom's habits and tried to learn from them.

They made a vow that they would not be like their mom – they would not drink or go out or ever tolerate any abuse, physical or mental, from any man. They also vowed not to have kids early; they remembered the resentful look in their mom's eyes when she couldn't go have fun and be irresponsible like she wanted. Owena and Thomasina did not want to take their failures out on the kids and blame the children for being "stuck." The kids felt that resentment.

The girls were half right.

As fate had it, both of them did have kids early, just like Dottie. But the part that they got right was that both of them left abusive, older boyfriends. They were also right that the children would not "hold them back"; they emancipated themselves legally, and took themselves to Haskell to better themselves at the age of 16. The girls said that they left from living under their mom's roof because, according to them, they felt like they were "out on their own anyway" since they were 11. Evidently, their mom was never around because she was always out partying or pursuing a man that didn't want her; basically trying to live the youth that she lost. The girls said that they had "no place to go but up" and "couldn't rely upon anybody *other than themselves*," so what did they do? They decided to become drug and alcohol counselors with Masters' degrees.

These young Indian girls showed that anybody, even the most vulnerable, young, teenage mothers, could drag themselves out of the deepest holes. Even when everybody gives up on them.

Mike snapped out of this memory and focused himself back into Professor Hed's office.

"...Professor, I've seen the resilience, the resourcefulness and the strength of Native people in tough situations. I've watched young Indian mothers who were only 16 or 17 years old and were completely poor and without resources; those young mothers were born to *other mothers* who had them at 16 or 17 years old themselves, and their mothers were also poor and without resources! AT LEAST two generations of teenage motherhood. I documented those incredibly vulnerable, yet incredibly resilient women in my paper; yet, you tell me that my paper was 'poorly reasoned.' Professor, with all due respect, you haven't seen the living conditions that many of these folks have overcome."

Mike paused and looked for the Professor's reaction. None. So he continued, "I've interviewed those incredible women and talked to them. I asked them exactly how did they overcome all the people like you – the liberals who say that Indian people cannot do anything for ourselves? How did these strong people resist those who say that we're doomed to mediocrity and self-destruction? How did they completely change their family's legacy and make better lives for themselves and their children despite the low expectations and intergenerational dysfunction? It was crazy, Professor, because in that short time span, I saw an entire social experiment on how poverty, dysfunction and abuse replicate themselves *intergenerationally.* Indian people are the human ant farm – reproduce quickly, live in small communities, and die early. Yet, I've watched young people, like these two young mothers, take control of their lives in the midst of incredibly vulnerable situations and say, 'I'm not going to raise my child like this. I'm going to pursue school – even though people like Richard Hed say that I cannot, that I should not – and I'm going to teach my child and my younger siblings and nieces and nephews, also the products of young mothers, that they *must* pursue their dreams."

Professor Hed sat there quietly. He pondered Michael's dramatic dismount for a little while. "Of course there will always be anomalies, Mr. First Rider. That doesn't prove anything," Professor Hed rebutted.

"It proves that your so-called anomalies *can* happen, Professor. My research proved that Indian women – much like the first generation of Holocaust survivors – when you take away all excuses, infrastructure and support network, *will* excel. They'll prevail. It was not *just* Owena and Thomasina; I documented lots of them. Now, granted, not all of them will do well. Of course not; that's unrealistic. But so what? Not every single descendant of the Holocaust survivors that I tracked excelled either. But the numbers went *way* up when those young ladies took away their excuses and decided that success was the only option. That's a fact – if you choose not to acknowledge that fact because it contradicts your books, so be it. It's a fact nonetheless. The fact is that a person's survival instinct *only* kicks in when their *very existence* is jeopardized. The programs that are in place for Indian people as well as all the millions of excuses – especially the biggest excuse that you folks make, the 'intergenerational trauma' excuse – keeps Native people from hitting the bottom. Native people's very existence is not jeopardized in the same way that Jewish people's existence was after the Holocaust. Therefore, these subsequent generations of Indian people simply do not have the survival instinct that Jewish people do. It's that simple; it's not because Jewish people are smarter or more talented or whatever. It's simply because their survival instinct kicked in because they had no excuses. Us, on the other hand, we *love* our excuses."

Professor Hed looked intrigued. "Fair point, about the survival instinct. Perhaps there's something to be said for a people's very existence being threatened. Seems drastic, but it makes sense. Still... what about suicide in Indian Country? Surely that must be the result of intergenerational trauma."

End Part 3

T R A U M A
(Part 4 of 4)

$\longleftrightarrow$

The Professor continued. "See, Mr. First Rider, we read one of my books in class. I believe that the third chapter is the section that deals with Native suicide. I truly think that the chapter has one of the singular best discussions of how intergenerational trauma deeply affects the Indian community. See, the most poignant and darkest, obviously, manifestation of that intergenerational trauma is the *incredible, horrific, and disturbing* numbers of Native Americans that commit suicide." Professor Hed grinned at Michael, as if he knew that he "got him." He was in his comfort zone. He knew that he was on strong ground here – that he was one of the few recognized experts on suicides in Indian Country. Michael was outclassed, pure and simple, the Professor thought.

Professor Hed sat up, as if he were getting excited by this discussion, and turned to squarely face Michael. He leaned toward Mike and opened up an imaginary book. "Here, in fact, I know the passage. I think it's on page 87 of my most recent book, *'It's Not Our Fault (Did I Do That?).'* I remember like I wrote it yesterday: 'Suicides in Indian Country are the *direct result* of the unholy trilogy of 1) boarding schools, 2) relocation and 3) termination. Boarding schools stripped the spirits, relocation stripped the land, and termination split the people.' I think that passage sums it amazingly. Mr. First Rider, I'm going to make a bargain with you. If you can refute this statement in a reasonable, coherent and historically accurate manner, I will elevate your grade, magically, to an 'A.' What do you think about that?"

Mike sat, staring at his professor. He smirked, as if intrigued; if his mom were there, however, she'd know that his flaring nostrils gave away his anger. He was insulted. He *already* earned an "A"; he should not need to prove, audition, or otherwise show the Professor that he deserves this grade. Still, despite the Professor's ridiculous and stupid looking grin that gave away his confidence on this point, Mike knew that he could "beat" him. He knew that he had the answer. He just wasn't sure that Hed *deserved* the answer after all the money and time that he wasted supposedly learning about Indians. Instead, Hed should have taken a grand tour of all the reservations and sat in each and every reservation high school and talked to the kids and noticed the trends amongst the kids. It's not rocket science – there's a very clear trajectory that commits suicide. Or if people would simply go to the Senior Centers and the weekly bingo, they would get it much better than these so-called "scientists" do – there is no conspiracy.

But his stubbornness would not allow him to do it. It was the same stubbornness that caused him to *never stop* cursing at and spitting on the four Nazi skinheads who stomped him when he was in 8th grade; he was found naked with four teeth kicked out and spitting blood, but he would not stop calling them "white trash" and "albino monkeys." His stubbornness made him forego his graduation ceremony from high school when the principal told him that he could *not* attend the ceremony in traditional garb, or as his principal called it, "his costume." His mom gave him the choice and he said that he would rather "swallow his blood than swallow his pride."

That stubbornness began to creep up here.

Mike could have easily told the Professor about the regression analysis that he did, and that based upon that analysis, "boarding schools," relocation and/or "termination" could NOT be the reasons for the massive suicides in Indian Country now. Impossible. "In fact," Michael thought, "the generation of Natives – according to the numbers – that suffered *directly* from boarding schools, relocation and/or termination did not commit suicide at nearly the rate that Native young people do now. Specifically, in 1979 Native suicide rates were 1.5 times the national average; today, we are more than double that, committing suicide 3.3 times more than the national average. Therefore, our suicides have *increased* instead of decreasing the further in time that we get away from boarding schools, relocation and termination. Yet we use those historical events as excuses for our behavior even *more* than before." Michael looked up at Hed's portrait of Quanah Parker and Goyathlay and shook his head. "Our strong leaders – our warriors NEVER used these things as an excuse to take their own lives. Geronimo fought like only an Apache could to maintain his way of life, and the government eventually captured him and made him completely change his way of life. Turned him into a farmer. And no suicide. Quanah Parker was a warrior amongst warriors, fighting and killing and doing whatever was needed to preserve his people's way of life. When his 'battle' days were over and he was relegated to the reservation, he still fought the encroachment of the white mindset, not giving into monogamy and Christianity. He also had his way of life stripped from him in front of his very eyes, and he did not commit suicide. They were warriors."

But Michael did not want to tell the Professor any of these truths.

"But the Professor would not get that. Indian people, who grew up with these things around us, get it. We know what the problem is, although most of us are not willing to say it. I'm not going to tell him. I don't want him to get 'it.' I'm not sure if he deserves to get it," Michael thought. He stood up and started to gather his things. The Professor, still boldly facing Michael, now leaned back curiously. "He does not know anything about warriors, or Native people. He only knows books. And he will continue to write misinformation until someone stops him. He doesn't get that suicide is not the problem, just like alcoholism is not the problem, just like child abuse and violence against women are not the problems; they are only the symptoms of a much bigger disease. He gives that disease strength every time he makes excuses for Indian people – it's like if you don't go to the doctor when you're sick because you're scared of the diagnosis. You don't want to face the diagnosis – and these people keep telling us we don't have to face the music. And they're lying to us. They're lying to us and they are killing our kids. They keep telling us that we have no control to stop this demon of suicide, and they're lying to our faces. They gotta be stopped. HE'S gotta be stopped. He needs to understand that he *causes* the very problem that he writes about – the type of person who convinces *us* that we cannot help *us*. That we cannot find the answers within."

Mike did not speak. He took his binder. He opened the door. He wanted to physically hurt the Professor. He wanted to protect the young ones from these people who tell Natives that they will never again perform nobly and be the best at something because of these transgressions that occurred hundreds of years earlier. He wanted to cry. Instead, he turned to face Professor Hed – eyes watering, bottom lip trembling – and stared into his eyes for ten seconds. Then he walked out of the school and went home.

End part 4

TRAUMA EPILOGUE

The next morning, as usual, Professor Hed opened his email:

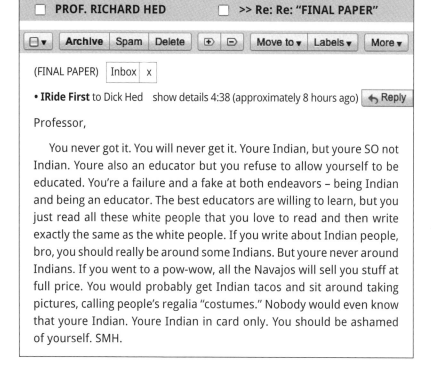

PROF. RICHARD HED   >> Re: Re: "FINAL PAPER"

Archive | Spam | Delete Move to ▾ | Labels ▾ | More ▾

(FINAL PAPER) | Inbox | x

• **IRide First** to Dick Hed show details 4:38 (approximately 8 hours ago) ↰ Reply

Professor,

You never got it. You will never get it. Youre Indian, but youre SO not Indian. Youre also an educator but you refuse to allow yourself to be educated. You're a failure and a fake at both endeavors – being Indian and being an educator. The best educators are willing to learn, but you just read all these white people that you love to read and then write exactly the same as the white people. If you write about Indian people, bro, you should really be around some Indians. But youre never around Indians. If you went to a pow-wow, all the Navajos will sell you stuff at full price. You would probably get Indian tacos and sit around taking pictures, calling people's regalia "costumes." Nobody would even know that youre Indian. Youre Indian in card only. You should be ashamed of yourself. SMH.

But I *am* Indian and so I have to set you straight about your thoughts on MY people. I have no choice but to educate you because I can't let you just continue doing what you're doing without showing you any different. Id be doing you a disservice, as well as all the white people who read your writing (do you *really* think that an Indian is going to read a book called "Young Native Man: Not Malicious or Mischievous, Only Mistunderstood?"). I know you'll be too much of a coward to reveal this email, but Im gonna leave that on your conscience and haunt you and youll remember this email forever. And if someone ever finds this email? You better make sure that you delete this, burn the computer then delete the email account, because if someone ever finds, it you'll have a lot of 'splaining to do, Lucy!!

Now, about your stupid ideas. Man, where to begin? Do you <u>really</u> think that boarding schools, termination and relocation are the reason why we young Native men kill ourselves so freely?? LOL. Youre an idiot. You couldn't be more wrong, Prof. And please note that I said "young Native men," because Native women dont kill themselves. At least, they rarely kill themselves. Suicide is a YOUNG NATIVE MAN's disease, in the same way that AIDS is a gay man's disease, even though we dont want to say it. Were too nice. But it IS ours and it has nothing to do with your stupid reasons. I mean, Im sure that at sometime, some lonely Indian punched his own clock because he was lonely and wanted to get away from Flandreau or Chemewa. But that's not usually the case – usually it has nothing to do with any of those reasons and only a white person that feels guilty about what theyve done to Indians would think that boarding schools, termination and/or relocation makes suicide happen. Now Professor, I hate to tell you this, but youre not white. Granted, you might as well be cause you think like a white person. But no matter how hard you try, youre not white.

The real deal is that young Indian men have no voice. We have no outlet. Therefore we have no choice. There. That's the reason that we kill ourselves, brilliant professor. No other reason. We are the only group that has everybody else speaking for us, like we are a museum exhibit sitting behind a glass case. We have everybody else who wants to speak for us, as if we're completely incapable of speaking. When white liberals walk by the glass, case they give us sad eyes like we're the bunny rabbits in the pet store window (remember that kid's song, "How Much Is That Doggie In The Window?" That's us, Professor. People want to adopt us, sponsor us, *save* us. But nobody wants to know us). If white people don't want to adopt us, every other white person expects us to be drunk 24/7. That's no exaggeration, Prof – they *literally* expect us to be drunk 24/7. THEN...to top it all off, we have supposed-Indians like you who tell us that we cannot do anything and should be absolved for any of our crimes – whether were dirty pedophiles or drunks – because we "cannot control ourselves" because of intergenerational trauma. We are completely powerless.

You really painted us into a corner there, ennit Chief? No voice, no outlet, no choice.

But that's not enough. We're not only hopeless, according to you, but we're also helpless to do anything about it, ennit?? We cannot make our lives better. We are incapable. All we can do is go through life having babies, being drunk and die prematurely. That's no kinda life, professor. I don't want to go through life always explaining myself, telling people why I was able to "make it off the rez" and that. I don't want people looking at me like I'm "special," like I'm the one Indian that was able to do right and everybody else did wrong. That's too much pressure. That's dishonest. That's not me.

So Im gonna help you out with one more statistic about Indians that you can use, Professor. Heck, Ill even present it to you like a problem and you can put it in a pop quiz to your students. Now, the truth is that I know that you wont tell this particular statistic when you talk to white people and you wont present this question to the mislead students in your class. But you should. And if you ever do get brave or real or Indian enough to tell the truth and tell this fact, I want you to tell the truth. This is the truth:

The reason that young Indian men commit suicide is because people like you convince us that we will never be able to speak for ourselves. You know that for a fact because you had one student – Mike First Rider, a former student of yours – who never went to boarding schools, was not the product of relocation and his tribe never dealt with termination. He was not hopeless, helpless and did not feel worthless. He was a straight "A" student studying for his Master's Degree with yuppie parents. He was not hopeless, helpless or worthless. He was voiceless. And sick of being voiceless...and that part, Chief, has not changed one bit since the days when the fake, Indian Agent-appointed "Chiefs" spoke and signed treaties for all of us voiceless Indian people. Those guys were hang-around-the-fort sellouts speaking for us, just like you. Boarding schools, relocation and termination changed throughout the years – in most situations they went away. But sellouts speaking for us and stealing our opportunity to give a REAL Indian voice has not changed or disappeared. We still have to deal with you sellouts that do the wild west shows just so that you can give white people the exact picture that they want to believe about us Indians. That picture is incorrect. Still, as long as people like you keep pushing that image – that we are just victims – just like the wild west shows, thats what white people will continue to believe.

My death contradicts that. I am not a victim. I could do anything that I want. Except speak for myself, because sellouts like you are so quick to jump and speak for us. My death is my sundance for the real Indians – it is my flesh offering for all of us young Native men who hope that one day fake ass Indians like you will develop some shame or conscience for giving all these white people the wrong picture about us. We continue to be screwed by you and your type, Chief. I want it on your conscience. I want to share this with your students and the world.

Heres a hypothetical question for you to use in your class, Chief: If a Native American Master's student one day got sick of his Professor spreading misinformation about Indian people and one day decided that his protest to the Professor was going to be that he commit suicide, how would that student choose to kill himself?
a) Overdose on pain pills.
b) Slit his wrists.
c) Jump off a bridge.
d) Leave the car running in the garage and die of carbon monoxide poisoning.

My guess? Unfortunately there seems to be an abundance of pain pills floating around Indian reservations. I dont know why, but it seems like the best answer to me so Im gonna stick with "a." You can correct me if I get it wrong.

Aho. Cracker.

Thanks,

Mike

"Self-determination means that we should expect to have to do it ourselves, stupid."

Mike never emailed again. Mr. Hed began doing his research for the summertime – reading all about himself. He loved to read the reviews of his new books and to see if there were any newspaper articles about his lectures. A few days after his last email with Mike, the professor googled himself and found his name mentioned in the local newspaper; of course he had to read it to see what good stuff they said about him:

Mr. Michael First Rider, 1980-2007

Michael "Mike" First Rider, 27, of Missoula, died Wednesday.

He was born to the late Aloysius and Ramyrna First Rider in Pablo, Montana. His parents worked hard to put themselves through college to set an example for their sons to follow. They both received their B.A.s from Salish-Kootenai College.

Mike furthered his parents' educational goals. His family took school seriously and so did he, graduating as Valedictorian for his high school class, and at the head of his class in Undergraduate at Stanford University. He then went to fulfill his dream – study Master's level work with renowned Native American Professor Richard Hed. He loved to learn, as his family loved to learn – he thought that education could save Indian people. Michael wants to send a special acknowledgement to Professor Hed for necessitating that message and suggests that if anybody has any questions why he felt the need to end his life early, to ask Dr. Hed.

In lieu of flowers, the family is requesting that donations be made out to Missoula Children's Charity.

A viewing will be held at 7 pm Friday at Valley Funeral Home. Burial will be held at 1 pm Saturday at the family cemetery.

I had a dream of a beautiful woman
She stripped off her dress
In the place of her stomach was a casket
Bottles of arsenic for breasts
Her face was magnificently featured
Skin that Nature smiled upon
And God blessed
She was a bronze-colored dime that reeked of death

I woke up in a cold sweat

That was an odd dream.
I thought nothing more about it
Just got up and went to work.

It was Friday in the winter
Like usual my man J hit me up right about noon
"Yo kid, be ready for tonight – 10 o'clock comes around soon
I know you've got your hot fit ready
To make the ladies swoon
But I've got mine too
Purple Label, Farragamo, my hair freshly groomed"

I simply said "you know this man – I'll hit you back in awhile."

Went about my job at Spacely Sprockets – this mindless 9 to 5
I find this work so unrewarding
I make a living at the cost of being alive
Typed five thousand words,
Drank coffee
Defragged my hard drive
I can't even focus on this stuff

Just thinking about tonight.

Got off work – drove home
My studio castle awaits.
To watch TV and lift weights and wait for my Friday night date
With destiny
Yeah child!
I don't want no scrubs tonight
Just want someone to rub me the right way
I want her face cute and her body tight
Stacked like the New York Yankees
Or the Miami Heat
Hit this little hot mami off on the first night
Maybe do the same thing next week.

That's right!
Call me a player, player.

Creed cologne on my clothing
Nivea lotion on my face
Jump in the BM 10 pm my den of debauchery awaits
And I'm just scanning the crowd
The music's crazy loud
My man J is at the bar talking to a chick
One that I don't think he'll be very proud of
When he wakes up in the morning
And rubs his eyes like a little kid
And looks over at the whore in horror
And wonders about the horrible things that he did
But that's not for now...

Right now
We're A Night at the Roxbury with melanin
My adrenaline is pumping
At eleven o'clock I meet a little Latina
Who's shaking her backside
So fly that I provide her
With whatever drinks she wishes
Grey Goose and Remy

My alcohol game is vicious
Now she says she wishes for her
And I to be alone
Of course that's not a thing
I type some letters into the phone
Text message J – "hey bro, I'm off – you know how I do"
Give pounds to my boys as I leave
You guys also know what I'm about to do.

Got to her house
You know what happened.
We both had a wonderful time that night
Said we'd stay in contact – of course we didn't
We had nothing in common
I'd just see her from time to time at the club.
We'd make eye contact
Give each other a fake smile
And quickly turn away.

Then one night
About three months later
I can't really be sure because the weekends kinda blurred
But at a different club on a different night
We danced together
I end up going back home with her
In the morning when we got dressed
And we both got ready to tell each other our lies
That we'll call each other
And that we've just been busy
She looked at me and she started to cry

I said "what's wrong, baby?"
She explained to me
She met this other guy
And did the same thing she did with me
Went home with him that same night
I said "You don't need to tell me this, baby
I don't judge you
Plus,

We're all just having fun right?"
She told me to shut up
And went on.

Through tears she told me that she left the club
Stumbled out to his ride
She could tell that he had been drinking too much
Still
He lived just a short ride
From the club and she was sure it'd be okay
But when they began to drive
They hit a small patch of ice on the road
The car began to slide
Crashed into a telephone pole
Minor bleeding, bumps and bruises
Thank God they were alright
But when she went to the doctor
He said that he wanted to take a look inside
A mere formality
But
He noticed more blood
Looked worried
Told her that this cannot be right
Told her "Ma'am, did you know you were pregnant?
I hate to tell you this, but your baby died."

Then she looked up at me with big red eyes
And said, "That baby was yours."

And I saw this beautiful woman
Who had stripped off her dress
In the place of her stomach was a casket
And bottles of arsenic for breasts
Her face was magnificently featured
Skin that Nature smiled upon and God blessed
A bronze-colored dime that reeked of death

2111

She saw the pictures, and simply could not see the resemblance. At all. Granted, some of her family members/friends told her that they could see the resemblance and the specific characteristics. "Yes, you definitely have a Tlingit jaw – I can see it in the pictures of your family."

But she took such praise/observations with a grain of salt. They cared about her. They knew that she felt insecure about this. It was very likely that they simply told her what she wanted to hear – what she *needed* to hear.

See, Winona grew up looking at all of the pictures of her family, past and present. Those pictures, in her words, were the "real Natives" in her family. She was fascinated by the pictures of the "real Natives" and constantly compared herself to the pictures. In the past few years, Winona grew increasingly curious about how she could look so incredibly different than the picture of her great-great grandmother. She bore almost no resemblance to her great aunties either – her grandmother's sisters. It didn't seem to make sense. She was a direct blood relation. Moreover, Winona *was* an enrolled member of the Tlingit Tribe – she was official. Still, her grandmother looked much more authentically "Indian" than she did, and it wasn't only the labret that she wore in the chin or the brownness of her skin. It wasn't just the shell earrings that her grandmother wore or the button blanket draped over her.

She just looked different. Her grandmother was beautiful. She was the epitome of "strong" and "Native"; Winona, even when she dressed up in Tlingit regalia, looked like a bad karaoke impersonation of her beautiful and regal grandmother.

She is not at all the same as the pictures that she saw from only a few generations ago.

She had some suspicions why. But those suspicions didn't explain everything.

For example, Winona read about how, in 1994, one-third of Natives married outside of their race. That was a lot of intermarrying, and that intermarrying very likely led to many children. It made complete sense that those children of intermarriage – now fairer-skinned and oftentimes living outside of their own homelands – sought acceptance in their new surroundings. Those new surroundings were often within white communities. That process, multiplied several times over several generations, obviously contributed heavily to the dilution of her blood and features.

She wondered why those people – her ancestors, who looked so "real" and beautiful – married outside their race in numbers so much higher than every other race? How could they not want to be with other brown, beautiful and "official" Indians? If she had the opportunity, she surely would be with one of those handsome and brown Tlingit men! Heck, she wouldn't discriminate – she'd be with a handsome, strong and brown Lakota, Blackfeet or Cree boy, too!

She wondered if her ancestors understood the effect that all of this intermarrying and cross-pollination would have upon their descendants. She suspected that her ancestors did not have *any* idea that their descendants – Winona and her generation – would have severe identity issues because of their European features and American Indian/Alaska Native enrollment number. No, her ancestors could not have known that this younger generation had no clue how they were supposed to act as Indians, what she was supposed to say when someone told her, "You don't look like a Native." Indeed, she surely didn't feel that she matched up with the images of "Native."

Nobody else thought that she matched up with those images either. It was like a guy who looked Asian saying that he was black – it just didn't make sense. Everybody else also saw those pictures of the regal and brown-looking Natives. Those people realized that

Winona, as well as her friends who also identified as "Native," looked different than the pictures. Her friends pointed it out from time to time – not in judgment, but in honest observation. They realized that this current generation of Natives paled, literally and figuratively, to the older generations. Her friends knew that she was Native, or came from Native people, but they didn't understand why she didn't look it.

Winona didn't understand it either.

There were still a few Natives who fit the prototype. Those folks were the "throwback Natives" – the bronze-colored men and women with almond eyes and jet-black hair. That throwback look was very rare now; indeed, a very popular cosmetic surgery package was the "Santa Fe Package" with lifted cheekbones, eternally tanned skin, electrolysis to remove all hair, permanently blacken the hair, and narrow the eyes. As an additional option, the Santa Fe Package would also shrink the size of the calves to have "chicken legs" for an additional fee. Winona could not afford the Santa Fe Package. Instead, Winona and her friends worshipped those few throwbacks like gods – collecting their magazines and watching their movies as most of those throwbacks were involved in entertainment.

See, in this technology-driven year of 2111, things like churches, schools and libraries are obsolete because of social networking technology. As such, there is a large movement to bring back "old school values," real conversation and handwriting. Cursive handwriting is at an incredible premium. In 2111, people began to romanticize an earlier time before holographic phones and air-breathing batteries, and even rotary telephones and electricity. People longed for simplicity. They looked back, nostalgically, at the era approximately 250 years ago – around 1855 – when homesteaders moved westward, the Great American War was fought, and Native American treaties were signed. Recognizing the draw of the noble and misguided savage, movie producers now made lots of movies about these treaty times. The throwbacks typically played the Indian roles, signing the treaties, explaining to their people (usually the other tribal members were CGI because there are not enough brown-skinned Natives to fill these scenes) the benefits of the treaties and then taking the lion's share of the spoils for themselves.

Indian movies were HUGE. Next to science-fiction movies about clean air and water, Indian-themed movies were the next biggest draw in 2111.

Winona would think, "God, those throwbacks are frickin' beautiful. I would pay any amount of money to have their Indigenous seeds swimming in me and have their kids." But she didn't see any of herself in these throwbacks. Therefore, she knew that her kids would look even *less* "real Native" than her.

When she told other people that she was Native, she could tell that they didn't believe her. She understood why – they saw the throwbacks and judged her according to them. Still, that was a strange standard. There were approximately eighteen million Natives in the United States, and most of them looked a lot like her because the interbreeding was rampant. In 2011, most Natives had light brown hair, and fit the description of what people in the 20th and 21st century called "white people." However, since use of the terms "white people," "black people," "Indian," "Oriental" and "Mexican" were officially arrestable as "hate speech," she really didn't know *who* she looked like.

She just knew that she didn't look like her grandmother.

Her friends believed that she was Native – she just wasn't sure that she believed herself. She knew that she did not look like her ancestors or the throwbacks. Therefore, she wondered, "Am I *really* Native?"

She was likewise insecure about her knowledge of "Native things," whatever that meant. For example, she knew nothing about her language. Nobody did, not even the throwbacks. She did read about the early 21st century efforts to save Native languages from extinction by a few dedicated and vigilant Indian people. Alas, it was already too late – in 2009, Native people had already lost one-third of all Native languages and were not willing to take drastic steps to save this most precious of resources. She read about how few of the tribes or Native organizations seemed to really care all that much that the remaining 190-something Native languages were in danger of disappearing forever. Instead, tribes spent their time giving away free money to their tribal members so that those tribal members could buy new cars and televisions and drugs and lots of sugary foods instead of preserving languages. Now, most of the descendants from those tribes can't even say "hi" in the language of the tribes to whom they say that they belong.

Those young Natives are lost. Just like Winona. They look nothing like their grandparents, talk nothing like their grandparents. Still, they say that they are members of the same tribes as their grandparents.

Strange.

Winona's in exactly the same boat – she's not judging. She surely doesn't know any words from her language. She can read a few, but doesn't know how they're pronounced. In fact, she doesn't know a lot about Indians, including what makes her different than every other person on the planet. She knows that she has a Certificate of Indian Blood, but that may as well be a Costco card because she's a white-looking girl who doesn't know her language. She does what she can – she represents loudly and has bumper stickers and sweatshirts and shell earrings and hats that proclaim her as "Native." Still, this young Tlingit woman truly has no clue what "Native" or "Tlingit" means, just like nearly every single Native person in the United States has no clue what "Native" means in 2111.

I
believe wholeheartedly in ghosts

I
remember the first time
I
Spoke with this man
On Second and Pike
He was Native, homeless and stink
I tried to avoid him
As I did the rest of the homeless Skins
Make my friends think all Indians do is drink

BUT
He saw me put my head down
"Hey chief!"
I tried to dismissively slip him 50 cents
He refused my donation with a wink

AND
Some words
Mischievous smile
"Brother I want your time
Not your dimes
You'd be more generous if you just listened to what I think."

I
Exhaled deeply
"Okay, alright man
But I have to go."
I was trying to just bounce – begone – get out of there and get to work.

HE

Looked at me – really looked in my eyes
"Little brother
Understand your privilege
For a second really try
See
Polite society doesn't say so but
You and I are different.

YOU'RE

A person I'm a phantasm that people walk by
Folks pretend they don't see me
Hear me
When I say "Hi"
People get scared
Pretend they're reading "The Stranger"
Turn iPods on high
Put their heads down
Just like you did
"Uh, oh – that old Indian drunk guy."
A terrifying reminder of this city's racist roots
Politicians would love to deny
When all the Natives were kicked out of the city
So we had to sneak back
A fact that causes Seattle's liberals to cry
In sympathy
Still they pass me and sigh
And still cannot bring themselves to talk to me
As they return to their warm
Dry
Homes on Capitol Hill or Queen Anne
And spend 6 bucks on a bag of organic sour cream and onion chips from
Trader Joe's."

"YOU

blend in
No disrespect little brother
But you're a federally recognized, brown-colored white man
I am a ghost

A relic
A direct descendant of the heartbroken Natives
Suffered the greatest disrespect
Kicked out of our own home
Genocide
Anonymity
Removal to reservations
Now
I rattle my change and try to get these peoples' attention
But they're so highly superstitious they're afraid to even mention
The old drunk Indian
"Just look in the other direction and it'll go away
Pretend you do not see him and he won't see you."

I
was fascinated
Because I knew that he was right.
I looked at my watch
I was late for work
But I was actually communing with a ghost
Sidewalk Ouija board
Someone dead and forgotten to the world
Even his family didn't know he was alive.

AND
He continued.
"I always had harmless intentions
Yes
I tired of the disrespect
But what could I do?
It's weird
Bro
But I realized when they fear us
Is
The only time that real people hear us
Acknowledge the spirits
Even though we're always here
Walking every day
Dr. Malcolm Crowe.

FOR
example,
I remember one morning
I showed up in some lady's reflection
She preened herself against the Macy's outside window
By the mannequins in the morning while she
Prepared to go to work
And I was just, just
Standing there, stretching yawning
I just woke up
But I was behind her and
Evidently
Looked like I was going to attack her
She screamed and fearfully acknowledged me
A ghost
But I screamed too
Just as scared
That was my bedroom and she could not understand why I would be there."

HE
laughed a tragic laugh and said
"I think I was more scared than her."

"STILL,
The police lights and sirens came fast
Those police must double as ghostbusters
They somehow had vision into the nether realms
Spotted me simply stretching behind this lady
And I soon was overwhelmed
Boots and clubs and tasers
Broke my silent morning
I just wanted some coffee
But they had other plans.
Tackled me to the ground
Scraped my chin on the concrete
Put my arms behind my back
Face into the sidewalk
Chipped my two front teeth

Such violence to my face my cheeks turned violet
Violated my small sense of peace
Split my cheek and tongue so I could barely speak out for them to stop
STOPPIT!!! PLEASE I'M SO WEAK!!
I CANT EVEN FIGHT BACK – I'VE BARELY EATEN TWO MEALS THIS
WEEK!!!"

I
woke up
It was dark.
In writhing pain
Wanting to die
Wanting to take a million pain pills like Brett Favre
Never come down from my high.
I'm not a vain creature still I couldn't believe what I saw
When I looked into the Macy's window
Those peace officers broke my jaw
Footprints on my forehead
My two front teeth missing
Patch of hair ripped out of my head
The skin on my chin rubbed raw
I cried."

THE
homeless man reached up to his forehead
Pulled back his hair
Showed me the scars.

"LATER
I spied the same lady coming out of the Macy's door
She laughed loudly into her cell phone as she walked by
Didn't notice my blood on the ground directly outside of the store
I stood barely four feet from her
Almost exactly the same distance as before
But she didn't pay any attention to me this time as she walked away
And I limped to get a close glimpse of her through half-shut eyes.
She strode toward the Metro
Saying her "goodbyes" loudly
I felt my heart beat rise
Didn't even realize that I almost died because of her

But I didn't.
And she didn't care either way.

STILL
I disguised my anger
The fact that I despise
This cruel yuppie
Who paid no attention
While the police baptized me
With blood, boots and clubs
As mere drunkenness
The police already tried
To vanquish me one time today
I thought it more wise
To instead sit in this infinite impotence
Of perceived inebriation
This powerless stance
As a figment of Westlake shoppers' imagination
Occasionally they think that they spot the apparition in the corner of their
eye
But behold
Upon another glance
It was only a bum.
A ghost."

WE
became friends.
I could not pretend that we ate dinner and watched games.
But friends nonetheless – we talked as equals.

OUR
conversations went like this for years
Whenever I'd walk by
He'd smile say "Hi Chief"
I'd say smile and say "Hi."
I'd buy him some hot tea
A cheap meal
Something fried
So we'd go inside Starbucks
Let him get dry

Cause they'd kick him out if I wasn't with him
"No Ghosts Allowed
Without a Human Standing By"
He'd tell me his stories
Before I met him
I would have called them all "lies"
But he showed me the scars
Where four teenagers split his head
Then ran off laughing
Or when these other guys
Thought that it would be a funny surprise
If they put broken glass in his bed
Which was only a few blankets in the alley
Still
It was a place to lay his head.

AND
I couldn't believe it.
But once again, he showed me the scars.

THAT
Was our relationship
"Hi Chief," smile, eat, "goodbye"
Some laughs, some tears, some hope, some sighs.

AND
Then
One day
No more "Hi/Byes"
No more stories
No more smiles
I wondered why
Did he have a new corner?
Three months passed by
I looked all over for him
I only knew his first name
But I've wondered why
And where did he go
Still
Who can you ask when a ghost dies?

HALF-FULL

She tapped her flip-flops lightly on the classroom floor. That was her nervous habit; she was not used to speaking up in class. But here she was, about to go against her nature, her genetics. She was going to speak up in class.

The young brown lady, dressed in full stereotypical "city community college" uniform – flip-flops, jeans and a Florida State University hoodie – raised her hand in response to the professor's question.

"Truthfully, I get a bit discouraged when I hear the 'negative' statistics. It seems like everyone – especially Indian people – *love* to emphasize how *bad* we have it. Almost like it's a point of pride." The young lady looked puzzled, furrowing her brow and pursing her lips, as if the "bad statistics" actually left a nasty taste in her mouth. She made the "I just drank orange juice after I brushed my teeth" look, realized that she was making a funny face, and stopped herself.

She was shy, after all.

The professor turned toward the young lady and looked a bit surprised at her response. He sized her up a bit and walked slightly toward her – it was wasn't a big classroom, therefore he could only walk a bit closer to her without looking aggressive. But he paced in front of the class, folding his hands into a triangle and looking contemplative. Professorly. "Ms. Kills Enemy, you are a member of a Native American Nation, no?" She nodded "yes." He continued upon seeing her agreement, "One thing to remember is that statistics are statistics. I don't make them up. I just integrate them into my teaching with no passion or pride. Now, I don't think it's anything to be ashamed of. It's not Native America's fault that it is in such a perilous position. It is high time, however, that mainstream America acknowledged the horrible situations that exist in Native American Nations. This is especially true, Ms. Kills Enemy, because it was America's colonialist practices that helped create those very situations. Native American Nations didn't create these situations – they are mere helpless victims in this colonialist, hegemonic regime. I know that the numbers are troubling. Maybe even depressing. Still, it's not your fault, Ms. Kills Enemy."

The professor was obviously very sincere about his beliefs. He didn't look much older than a student himself – and he wore largely the same uniform that the young Indian girl wore – flip-flops, baggy "Rex-Kwon-Do"-type purple pants, and a "Homeland Security" shirt now very popular at pow-wows with people who have no clue who the Indians on the shirt are. The professor also had his hair in a silly "Shirley Temple" bob that made his head look even skinnier than it was. He was, in a word, a "hippie."

Ms. Kills Enemy did not like hippies. She felt that they were counterproductive to Indian people. Plus, they tended to stink.

Ms. Kills Enemy – now billions of miles removed from her home reservation in this city community college – sat back, took a slow, deep breath and examined the white professor's condescending sympathy. He really didn't mean to be condescending, she thought, but he couldn't help it. He's simply a victim of his skin color and the baggage that goes with it – *always* thinking people of color are incapable of controlling their own destiny. *Always* thinking that Indians needed white people to make the "bad" things go away. She thought of her childhood – yes, there were certainly "bad" parts to her upbringing. She remembered being the mixed-girl, the half-breed girl, and all that being a half-breed entailed on her home reservation. She remembered getting threatened – "I'm gonna tune you up, you little white girl bitch!" – and worse, the threats actually being carried out. She still has the fingernail scars on her cheeks.

She also remembered, like it was yesterday, waking up for school in the house where her mom and aunties and a bunch of friends partied all night the night before. Maybe a friend died or her auntie got laid off, and they were all going to drown their sorrows together. Or maybe it was a happy time. Who knows? Who really cared?

Everybody was pissy and loud and obnoxious at her house. She'd try to hide in her room and play Nintendo or listen to Randy Wood or Shania Twain. When the morning time came, to her dismay, the house was *still* full of drunks. She got up, got ready, and stepped over drunk people passed out on the floor as if it were part of her normal routine. She'd jump over some, step around others and occasionally just stomp really, really hard on someone that she didn't like, someone who was particularly obnoxious, or a grown man who'd tried to make a pass at her. It was her game of "rez hop scotch." She remembers falling asleep to the sounds of drunk people singing along with Queen's "We Will Rock You," and thinking that it was raining outside because someone was peeing outside her window. She heard them whispering that they couldn't wait for the bathroom, and plus that "snakey bitch Laverne was talking bad about her." That night Ms. Kills Enemy woke up once when she heard her mom crying when someone started fighting. She heard her mom ask through tears, "Why do you guys have to get all ignorant? We were just in here having fun!"

Yeah, sure. Ok. There was certainly bad stuff. There was stuff that she wishes that she could forget, or hadn't experienced. No question.

She knew that kids were having kids on her reservation. She wasn't stupid. She didn't need the professor's statistics or fruity pants to remind her of that. Heck, she knew that Indian kids were having kids in the cities. She knew that sexual abuse is rampant back home; she also knew that unemployment was, in good months, at 50%, and that suicides are a modern pandemic. She knew all of this. In fact, she lived all this – she surely did not need some soft college professor with a bob tell her that.

She knew all of that. But she didn't feel that the "bad" numbers spoke for all of Indian people. In fact, she did not feel that it was even the biggest part, even though this professor seemed to think that it was the sum total of Indian people. Like Indian people did not have any hope. No. There was plenty to be proud of as an Indian woman. Lots. "We're getting better all the time," she thought. She did not need to be proud of the dysfunction and tell everyone about it.

She lived that dysfunction. Her family did too. She worked to move away from that dysfunction – to *not* be identified simply by her people's struggles. Yes, those struggles were a part of her life, but they did not define her. She wanted to get that smug sympathetic look off those white liberals' faces. She hated white liberals, like this fruit. She knew that guys like him only paid attention to poor people so that they could have a "Fight Club" rationalization for their own misery – to know that there *is always* someone doing worse than them. This sucker gave to charities and talked about poor people because it was like his own personal Testicular Cancer Support Group – they made him feel better about himself. Validated. Like he's not such a loser. The little African kid in Somalia with flies on his face or the 14-year-old Lakota boy who commits suicide makes it much easier for him to live with the fact that white people have ruled the world for over 500 years – the world is literally designed so that no white person should ever struggle financially or professionally – yet somehow this clown earns $32,000 a year.

He was wrong about Natives. He was wrong about "statistics." Statistics are not simply statistics. Statistics are animals, creatures, science projects gone awry. And like Frankenstein, pit bulls or child soldiers, those statistics can be beaten into submission, experimented on, ridiculed, sodomized and taught to kill. They are not objective, not empty vessels – people put their biases into those statistics. Therefore, when a racist gets hold of some statistics, he can make those statistics racist and show awful things like the Bell Curve or phrenology. Hitler was a statistics guy.

Garbage in, garbage out. What this hippie said was pure racist garbage. Problem is, some Indians have begun to believe the garbage.

She knew that Natives were not victims. Her grandpa taught her that Native people are never victims. Yes, at one time "the white man" controlled a good portion of Native peoples' fates. Fine. That was then. Now, the U.S. has a crumbling economy. Crime is out of control and there are significant signs that this is a decaying nation; the white, racist power structure is a failed experiment. People, like this professor, seemingly cannot even control their own fates anymore. White men like her professor – a megalomaniac who wants to accept blame for all people of color's suffering – want to feel powerful one more time. Like the good old days. So they pretend to be the cause of everything.

A God complex.

She wanted to fume and retreat to her quiet sulking, which was her tendency. But she was done fuming. She was done quietly sulking. She was done being quiet. She had to speak.

"Mr. Smallwood, you're wrong. In fact, you're dead wrong. Yeah, there's a million 'bad' statistics that show that we're struggling. But the fact is that we're getting stronger every day. Any idiot can look at the statistics with no critical thought and say 'Gee, there sure are a lot of unemployed Natives.' In fact, any idiot can look at the statistics and take them at face value. I've read, for example, some telling studies about white men's penis sizes.

"Still," she said, "I take those little things with a grain of salt. I know that it takes a slightly more nuanced and critical view to look at those same statistics and say, 'Wow, assuming those statistics are true, there are actually *employed Natives.* A lot of them! That simply was not the case in the recent history' See, 100 years ago we were literally about to be wiped off the face of the earth. There were about two hundred and fifty thousand Indians in North America. I guess at that point white people would have been able to take credit for our extinction. Now? There's a lot of us. And we have access to exactly the same schools, jobs and doctors that white people have. Now, if we mess that up, it's all on us. We Natives have 100% responsibility for ourselves and if we mess up, we mess up. But no white person can ever take credit for our mistakes again.

"We make our own statistics now – you show me a statistic that says that we have the highest percentage of suicides, and I'll show you one that says that we aren't even supposed to be in existence any longer to commit suicide. Give me a statistic that shows that we're struggling with alcohol, and I'll likewise provide you with a statistic that shows that we were supposed to go the way of the Dodo bird a LONG time ago. But we didn't. We're still here, and getting healthier every day. I'll be the first to admit that we are not perfect, but we're getting stronger. We are not victims. We are victors. Punk."

The rest of the class looked stunned. Then they started clapping slowly, like at the end of the "Revenge of the Nerds." A small tear appeared on Professor Smallwood's cheek and then he sneezed. The tear disappeared.

Ms. Kills Enemy received a "C+" in that particular class.

AKII
(A Love Story)

"miss lady, miss lady
do you believe in love at first sight?
or should I walk by again?

"No truly
Miss Indigenous
I've been feeling your vibe
Since time immemorial
Long before we were known as tribes
Or Native Americans or Indians or any of these other lies
That we subscribe to
That denies yours and my
True legacy as the original nitzitapi of this ksai-kum

"I guess what I'm trying to say is that, 'This really isn't first sight.'

I''n fact
Niin-sta
I've been scooping you since you first gave birth to this Earth
This land
Breast fed me with your flowing waters
Shaped the mountains with your hands
Matriarch of this continent
Earth wind and fire at your command
Lifespan is eternal
Hourglass turned sideways
No movement to your sand
Beauty and class are internal
No movement to your sand

"I guess what I'm trying to say is, 'Girl you look good for your age.'

Zero movement to your sand tho I know your life hasn't been a beach
There had to be problems before the first Napi-kwon landed on your beach

But
Now I find myself calling you 'bitch' acquired his profanity in my speech
Breached your confidence in my manhood leave my young ones for you to
teach
And
I know you're a bad woman
Ma
There's just some things that you cannot teach
And you shouldn't have to

"I guess what I'm saying is, 'I'm sorry.'
Because now when I see you with somebody not Nitzitapi I feel a sense of shame
Provided you with every excuse
Miss Lady
I know I'm mostly to blame
Desecrated your royalty yet you were loyal I can't say the same
Waited in vain for my love
Of course it never came
Provided me with gentle reminders of your blind affection every time that
it rained
Ignored for centuries needed a way to vent your frustration and your pain

"I guess what I'm saying is, 'I understand.'

"But
I'm begging for understanding too
Nii-nsta
I'm trying to be that niin-na
That man
That I should have been since long before time was called 'time'
Before 'husband' and 'wife'
I was simply yours and you were simply mine
I did not have to act as a man
Rather
Just followed Absti-doki's design
No need to try to be a man
Just walk in the way that the Creator defined
I think I can do that again

"So I guess what I'm saying is, 'Can I have your phone number?'

4 8

Junior decided that he was going to be different.

He remembers the exact night he decided; heck, he remembered the exact hour, the exact moment even. It was March 30th, 2003, while he watched the 11pm rerun showing of "Family Guy" on a non-premium cable station. This was his nightly ritual – lie down, eat his second dinner of the night (typically fried chicken from the local Town Pump or Sinclairs with a Shasta grape pop) and chuckle with the Griffins until he fell asleep on the couch. This particular night was one of the better "Family Guy" episodes; it was the one where Peter signed his life over so that he could get out of his medical bill and Death comes to get him. Death broke his ankle chasing after Peter and Death and Peter make a deal for Peter to not have to die then and leave his family behind.

Classic stuff. It insisted upon itself. But it was still funny, though.

Oddly, that particular episode sparked some profound thought in Junior, deep thoughts from a nonsensical cartoon with a talking dog. Still, the show did inspire a thought: Junior decided that it would be horribly sad to have to leave his family earlier than God intended. He didn't want to. It wasn't right, him leaving his family so early. But he knew that he was going down that route toward an early death – and chances were, unlike Peter Griffin, Junior probably would not be able to cut a deal with Death to stick around longer. Who knows? Maybe he could. He just wasn't convinced.

Either way, Junior decided that he didn't want to "follow the Indian man script" anymore; y'know, the script that predetermines that

Indian men are destined for a healthy childhood, fishing, running, playing basketball all the time, only to quickly deteriorate after their high school basketball careers into a pudgy mass of beer, fried foods and high fructose corn syrup. Or alternatively, the script says that the Indian man is going to die in a car accident because he didn't wear his seatbelt or die from cirrhosis on the streets of his local reservation.

Junior decided to throw that script away; that night he decided that he no longer believed in the ethnic Calvinism that seems to put Native men on a road to an early death almost immediately after the Indian boy's birth. Indeed, while watching "Family Guy" he realized that he had a compelling reason to change the script. His reason? He wanted his oldest son, Will, to be raised with his daddy – a gift that Junior never got. He wanted to babysit Will's children and get tired of them and wish that Will would hurry up and get home.

Most Indian men do not get to babysit their grandchildren. Rarely happens. The men in Junior's tribe are statistically unlikely to ever be able to babysit their grandchildren.

When Junior made his decision to change his life, Will was almost 10 years old; Junior was almost 40. In 8 years, when Will turns 18 and moves into legal adulthood, Junior will turn 48 and will probably be in bad physical condition. At that point, according to statistics, Junior only had a few years of life left to spend with his son and other children.

Maybe it was too late to change the trend for Junior. Perhaps it was simply the reservation's heartbreaking poetry. That is, the moment of a male child's entrance into adulthood coincides with his dad's passing into the next world, so that the boy needs to learn how to be a man all by himself. It seems like it happens all the time. No instruction, no mentorship on "how to be a man."

It was all so very Greek Tragedy – beautiful, yet ultimately heartbreaking. Junior never really thought about how sad and dysfunctional the whole cycle was. He just kinda took for granted that, like his father and most of his uncles, he would also die before his 50th birthday and a single mother would raise his children.

That's just the way it goes, right?

But he was thinking about it now, because of this "Family Guy" episode = deep thoughts from Peter and Stewie. He stayed awake for hours after the episode was over, immersed in his thoughts. Finally, at 3:14 AM, Junior rolled over on the couch, pulled the blanket over his head and fell asleep with the TV still on.

The next day it was still on his mind. He didn't remember what he'd dreamed – he wasn't much of a dreamer. Still, the number "48" kept popping up in his head when he woke up. He got ready for work and tried to figure out what "48" meant.

Junior went through the work day like an automaton, not able to fully engage in his work or with his co-workers. He ended up going home early because his supervisor thought that he must not be feeling well – why else would he refuse doughnuts? He got home before any of the kids made it home from school; when the kids got home, they did their chores and Junior just sorta spaced out watching them.

"They're so beautiful," he thought. "They deserve better." Junior looked over at Will sprawled out on the floor with his shoes off, playing with his Wii. His little man was so not so "little" anymore. He was 10 years old, and like Junior was going to be huge, probably 6' 2" or 6' 3". Still, even though Will was not small and fragile anymore, he was still young and delicate and *perfect*; he was everything that a father could dream of in a son.

He wanted both his mom's and his dad's attention at all times, so he always played sports hard. Will also did his schoolwork and chores well. He practiced his grass dancing. He even acted like Junior toward the younger kids – Will was always the authority figure, instructing the other kids how to shoot a jump shot better or write better cursive. When Junior was at work or in the other room, Will *was* the daddy. "He's the perfect son," Junior thought. "He deserves more than to be forced to become the man of the house at 10 years old. He deserves a father for a very long time."

Junior thought out loud. "That means I gotta be different. I can't do what everyone else does – obviously that hasn't worked too well around here. I'm gonna beat 48." Will looked up at his dad from the floor with a quizzical look. Then he turned back to his game of MarioKart.

The "Family Guy" episode about Death reminded Junior about a newspaper article that he read a few weeks before. He didn't know what to make of the story at the time, and last night, during "Family Guy," he didn't make the connection. But this morning he woke up and the article made all kinds of sense to him; the story was real, and literally predicted when he, and other Native men like him, were supposed to die. It was his Scrooge, "Ghost of Christmas Future" moment.

The newspaper article talked about how short Native men's life spans are and some of the contributing factors to their early demise. Of course, Junior had certainly heard all the numbers before. Still, he never really paid that much attention to the numbers – why would he? He was a young Native stud, with long hair and a big belt buckle, completely carefree and immortal.

This time, however, those numbers hit a little bit closer to home; they sent chills down his spine. Then, in a moment of clarity, as Will cheated his way to victory in Wario Stadium, Junior remembered why the number "48" was so significant – the article that he read said that he was supposed to *die* at 48. The prospect of leaving Will, his little man, as well as his younger daughter and son alone to figure out life by themselves in just a few years was unbearably sad to him. They needed their daddy's instruction, his loving hugs, and sometimes his harsh swats on the butt. But that article said that he should be gone by that time.

"I *have* to be different." Junior thought. "I owe it to my boy to be different."

He went online to look for the article – that was gonna become the motivation for him to change his life. He Google searched: he knew the particular article that he read came from the Centers for Disease Control or the Indian Health Services or one of those government agencies that love to talk about the horrible ways that Indian people die. Those agencies always show that Indian people are the very best at dying – better than anybody else in the country.

Here it was: the article quoted a bunch of doctors who said that men on the Pine Ridge Indian Reservation – his home for his entire life – only lived to be 48 years old; that was a full third less than the rest of men in the United States! An Indian doctor with the last name "Gupta" wrote the article so it had to be right!

It was right there in black and white. "48. I'm going to die," Junior thought. He thought back to his days in college and remembered how there was always a protest going on about saving tuna or dolphins or something, or kids in Malaysia wearing Levi's jeans or something like that. Then he thought that it was amazing and sad that human rights activists – these people protesting dolphins or tuna fish – as well as Natives and hippies and white people who thought that they were Natives, were not protesting in the streets and throwing Molotov cocktails to get Indian people better health care. This was the worst kind of human rights violation – "I have no right to live past 48," Junior thought. "The United States sends all this money all over the world – one billion dollars a month to Iraq – and there's homeless people, kids without health care at all, and Indians who have some of the worst health statistics in the western hemisphere, right here."

It was disgusting. It was hypocritical. It was also scary because he was quickly approaching his 40th birthday on May 3rd; Will had his 10th birthday on that same day. Therefore, Junior had roughly 8 years – if the statistic held up – to teach his son everything that he will need for his next 30 years, before his inevitable early demise. Either that, or Junior was going to have to figure out how we was going to live longer.

"That's a lot of teaching in 8 years. I think I'm going to try to stick around a bit longer."

Over the next several months, Junior became a student, a ninja, an anthropologist and a nutritionist all wrapped up into one. He started paying close attention to his surrounding community, what his friends ate, drank, when they went to bed, and if they exercised. He knew that lifestyle had a lot to do with the early deaths and that changing his lifestyle would be the first step in changing his fate.

To put it frankly, Indian men in this part of the country died early because, well heck, they lived like they wanted to die early. They didn't deserve to live long because they abused their bodies. He'd lived like that since he left college, and must now make a serious effort not to continue to live like that.

It came so easily; Sonic, Diet Pepsi, aspartame, fried foods, sugar, frybread and alcohol. He had so many diseases in his family, you'd think that they were the Russian Royal Family: diabetes, hypertension, heart disease, cancer, halitosis. The list went on and on, and most came back mainly to diet. So he worked hard to change it. Modifying his diet was not easy, but it was necessary. He gave himself one month to make small changes to it.

A few weeks later, he felt that he was starting to get a grasp on his diet. It wasn't perfect, but it was improving – he forced himself to drink water 4 times a day, and also to eat vegetables with every meal. Heck, he even stopped eating meat for one meal a day; while that may not seem like a big deal, Junior had a personal vendetta against meat and wanted to consume every bit of it in the world, animal by delicious animal. He was a one-man meat-eating machine! Taking meat out of one meal a day was a HUGE step for him.

Consequently, he began to notice slight changes in his physique and energy level; his muffin top diminished, his man-boobs shrunk. He didn't look the "Twilight Saga" guys *yet*, but at least his "Bud Light Saga" look faded. Now, he tended to make it to bed more frequently (instead of passing out on the couch in the middle of the night) and woke up with more energy.

Now that his diet was improving, it was time to work on a few other things. He began wearing seat belts. He *never* wore a seat belt before – he thought that seat belts were for sissies and for times when women drove. Now, he thought about how silly it would be for him to die in an otherwise routine car accident on the rez. He sighed sadly. He couldn't even recall how many cousins, friends, and uncles lost their lives prematurely to this seemingly miniscule thing. How many times did he get the call in the middle of the night to alert him to the bad news of a cousin who drove their truck into livestock or deer or elk on the highway? Silly. Sad. Of course they weren't wearing seat belts – it was almost against the law for Indian men out here to wear those. A 1,000-pound elk at 85 miles per hour? Never had a chance. His friends even joked about it, "Which white general killed the most Indians? General Motors."

When he started wearing his seat belt, he realized how unfunny that joke was.

He began wearing his seatbelt religiously. He made it a rule that if you got in his car, you had to put your seatbelt on – it didn't matter who you were. Many of his friends stopped riding in the car with him.

He didn't indulge some of the other ways that his friends indulged. He didn't have unprotected sex with many faceless partners on drunken nights out. Never happened. He also never used drugs and/ or cigarettes in his life. But like most Indian men, he dodged doctors appointments like it was a committed relationship; he didn't like to hear bad news and didn't like needles and honestly just generally disliked white doctors. His grandparents warned about white doctors. "They let our people die from smallpox and tuberculosis, baby. They stole our babies. Don't trust them. Watch them closely. Rely on Indian medicine."

He *did* watch them closely. He paid close attention when they gave his children inoculations or immunizations. He read about every procedure and medicine online and refused to give his children anything unless it "made sense." Still, he knew that doctors also had the capacity to heal and rescue. He knew that he needed traditional medicine. But he also knew that he needed Western medicine and sometimes antibiotics (for example, the time he got Chlamydia; he shuddered thinking about what the traditional cure was for that. Ouch.). He resolved that he would go to the clinic for a full medical checkup at least once a year.

"Family Guy" proved to be life-changing for Junior. It was going to make sure that he lived past that magical number 48. The research that he did in the next few weeks emphasized that Junior was not bulletproof, elk-proof, STD-proof or cirrhosis-proof; in fact, men from his particular tribe were quite the opposite. They succumb to those things at incredible rates, and Junior convinced himself that he would not do so. The way that he was going to ensure that, beginning at age 40, was to set out a plan that would work by *not* making drastic changes. He did not want to become a completely different person, a health nut, or religious. Instead, he decided that he would make slight modifications to his lifestyle that would put him on the right path to being healthier. His children deserved it. Will deserved it. Heck, he deserved it. There was no telling how good "Family Guy" would be in 10 years – it's getting better all the time.

He wanted to be around to see it.

Mama
When I open my mouth
Yet
Nothing comes your way
Except unfulfilled dreams and shy tense glances
Still seemingly with nothing to say
Please accept that
I've already said it all
And
Nothing at all simultaneously

See
My silence is golden
I've already married you in effigy
I conceptualize my commitment to you so effortlessly
It's innate
Like the way you inundate me with new feelings
Much too innovative for mere words
Brand new emotions send me reeling
Somewhere to the far right of hate
Extreme left of love
I can't explain these feelings
S-s-s-stuttering and stammering, and, and...

See what I mean?

These are pregnant pauses
Honest my aboriginal goddess
I feel not worthy to mumble
In your presence
Slightest essence of you
Makes my arrogant nature humble

Drop to one knee
Bow my head
Seek your blessing
Your balm of Gilead
Cleanse the transgressions that I'm not confessing
Because I cannot speak
Hail you.

My Madonna
I wish to be coddled in your palms
Yea tho I walk through the Valley of Solitude
You'll calm me with your Psalms
Salve my wounds and solve my problems
One touch from you can make me whole
Save me from my lonely purgatory
Restore and sanctify my soul
If I could only speak
But I cannot speak
I cannot speak
Therefore I cannot be forgiven
Therefore you won't hear me ask for your hand
Therefore I'll keep on living.
Without you.

PEE

"Look, I understand why <u>you</u> think that it was inappropriate. I get that completely. But at the same time, I want you to understand why it was necessary. It is important that you understand that it *was* necessary, and it still *is* necessary," she paused thoughtfully, "and unfortunately it will probably keep being necessary around here. Sad fact, but it's the truth."

She was obviously defensive. Still, you could tell that she thought that she was truly "right." She faced her interrogator head-on, with her eyes firmly fixed on his; she didn't appear afraid at all. In fact, she seemed very sober and cognizant of the seriousness of the accusations that she faced. Her body language also made it very clear that she was willing to suffer the consequences for her actions. She made it very clear that she would do exactly the same thing again if she were in the same situation – her body language was not penitent or regretful. Her shoulders were back and her jaw was clenched.

She continued, "Those kids have to learn, sir. That's a fact. My job is to teach; that's why you hired me, right or wrong?" The man nodded yes. "Exactly. So I'm not going to apologize for doing my job *too well*. How silly does that sound? 'I'm sorry for teaching your kids valuable life skills.' Sounds silly, don't you think?"

She looked directly into the eyes of her boss, the principal of the school. She realized that maybe she was sounding a bit "smartie." That wasn't what she wanted to do. She slowed her speech and quieted down a bit so she didn't seem insubordinate or flippant. Still, she *had* to be very clear that she truly believed that she was doing the right thing; therefore she reemphasized her point respectfully, "Sir, if nobody else will teach them, then I guess I have to teach them.

Or else someone else is going to have to step up and do it. Heck, I'll do it as community service if you fire me. That's fine. I can live with that. I won't even fight you on it. Just know that I'd do the same thing again ten times out of ten. I can live with you firing me. But I cannot live with me *not* doing my job and these little Indian boys suffering because of it."

The man sighed. He was the principal of this particular school – "Mr. Elk Teeth." Deep in his heart Mr. Elk Teeth knew that she was right – that she was simply addressing a problem that someone else created. Yes, this *was* a problem. Somebody did, indeed, have to take the initiative to make sure that this problem was addressed. Still, he was in a delicate position – he knew how sensitive the parents would be about something like this. He surely wasn't going to be the one to address this problem – he could just see the headlines, "Controversy at Tribal Kindergarten as Principal Holds Schoolboys' Pee-Pees." No, no, no – that couldn't happen. Mr. Elk Teeth has never been the "coolest" guy in the world. Still, he was *way* too cool for that headline.

The thought made him shudder.

Mr. Elk Teeth finally spoke, avoiding eye contact with the young lady. "Jen, I understand why you did what you did. Still, you have to admit this doesn't look good. At all. *You're* going to be the one to explain why you were helping these little boys pee. I understand your reasoning; I get it completely. But then, as all of us know, Jen, the people around here love to complain. Are they going to be the ones to fix the problem? No. Of course not, unfortunately. BUT, as we all knew would happen, the parents started complaining about *you* doing the job that they wouldn't do! Is that fair? Not one bit. Still, I have a big family and I can't afford to take the hit for you. I'm just not going to be the one to get fired or even sit on the hot seat on this one. Jen, I have four kids – I cannot lose my job. We had to schedule an emergency community meeting with all of the parents tomorrow at 11am. I hope that they're understanding of why you chose to do what you did, and I also hope that the meeting sparks a larger discussion within our community about parental responsibility. I hope it does. Still, Jen..."

Mr. Elk Teeth paused as if thinking about the consequences of his words very carefully. He finally looked into her eyes. "Fairly or unfairly, if those parents demand that I fire you, guess what? I'm going to have to fire you. I'll have no choice. This is a tribal kindergarten and I have to deal with these families for several more decades. I answer to them – they are my bosses. I hope that they see the intelligence in what you did. But I can't guarantee that. So the outcome of this event tomorrow might be that you'll have to look for another job, in which case I will surely utilize any resource that I have to help you find a great job. But before any of that happens, I'm going to give you a chance to explain to those parents, face-to-face, why you feel that it was appropriate to help all of those little boys pee."

Mr. Elk Teeth got up out of his seat, put on his jacket and walked past all the little kid artwork. There were beautiful little masterpieces of macaronis pasted into heart shapes, cotton ball snowmen and glitter elephants peppering his large office. When he arrived at the door, he paused. He opened the door and looked back at Jen. "I'll see you at 11. Good luck. I truly mean that. I think that you did the right thing. But sometimes the 'right' thing isn't good enough. I hope that the parents are reasonable and understand your wisdom. Still, young lady, I recommend that you be very well-prepared."

THE COMMUNITY MEETING
11:17am (Indian Time)
MULTI-PURPOSE BUILDING

Jen took a deep breath before she took her seat at the community meeting. She was nervous. She hoped that her voice did not shake. She was going to have to really focus to make sure that it did not. She didn't wanna cry. "Don't be a weak girl. You did the right thing," she told herself.

The room was huge – it sat approximately 2,500 people. Right now it was pretty empty; maybe 80 people overall. Still, the 80 people who were there did not look happy and the fact that the room was pretty empty did not make Jen feel any better. At all.

The crowd of brown faces, primarily women, looked at this young

Native lady angrily. They took their seats, glaring at her. They made no attempts to be nice or to look impartial – they already had their minds made up. "GUILTY!"

Mr. Elk Teeth felt the tension and walked past her without looking at her. He stood up on the little stage at the front of the Multi-Purpose Building and addressed the crowd: "Parents, I understand your frustration with the current situation. Believe me, I know you are concerned parents and do not want anything strange or improper to befall your beautiful children. I have not made my mind up about this situation; I definitely think that there was some questionable judgment, but I also understand that Ms. Jen has an explanation for her actions. Therefore, I believe that Ms. Jen deserves a meaningful opportunity to talk to the parents of this community and explain herself. Please, I beg you, keep this discussion respectful and please be open-minded. I know there are strong feelings about this. But this *is* an educational institution and we want our children to keep their ears and minds open. I ask that you do the same. Now, with no further ado, Miss Jen."

The young Native teacher stood up to address the angry crowd. Her voice sounded very hollow when she began, "Hello. My name is Ms. Jen." She looked at the microphone as if to check whether or not it was on. Mr. Elk Teeth indicated to her that everybody could, indeed, hear her and to go on.

"Sorry. I am your children's kindergarten teacher. I am from the Crow Nation, which is located in Montana. I also have family in Oklahoma in Kiowa territory. My daddy is Kiowa. I say that to point out that I'm Indian and I grew up around Indian people. I know how serious we are about protecting our kids. I assure you that I would never do anything weird with any of yours, or anybody else's, kids. But I have a job to do. And unfortunately," she paused and scanned the crowd to assess the risk of this next statement, "unfortunately, this is my first time meeting many of you even though I've taught many of your kids here for 3 years now."

There was a murmur in the crowd. Some of the ladies in the very front gave each other a disgusted look and whispered back and forth. Jen continued, "I know that some of you have very legitimate questions concerning my teaching style. I like that. I'm thankful that you're giving me a chance to answer those questions. Rest assured, I think that my teaching style is very necessary, otherwise I would never, ever take some of the actions that I have."

She was beginning to feel a bit better about herself now. She reminded herself that she was *right* – that she did the right thing here. She was ready, regardless of what the consequences were, to tell these people what they needed to hear. Then she sat down at the table on the stage. "Are there any questions?"

The crowd was shocked at her question. They felt like she was not being penitent enough. Of course there were questions! How could there not be questions? The ladies in the crowd looked at each other, as if seeking an explanation from one another. Then a short, chubby lady with a tight perm – her hair resembled Lionel Richie's in *"Dancing on the Ceiling"* – stood up and waddled to the microphone. She pointed at Ms. Jen on the stage. "Listen, you damn Crow, what the hell are you thinking touching my boy's penis?"

Jen looked out. It seemed like every other tightly permed, 5'3" 190 pound brown woman nodded her head "yes" as if they had exactly the same question. Jen could not help but chuckle inside at the uniformity of the curls AND the nod. But she kept her face serious. Mr. Elk Teeth motioned for the crowd to calm down and reminded them that she was entitled to answer the question. The short, permed lady stood at the microphone glaring at the young teacher, waiting for an explanation.

Surprisingly, the young teacher sat at the table on the stage and calmly nodded her head "yes" as well. She didn't get defensive at all. Instead, Ms. Jen looked out at the crowd wistfully and pursed her lips. She spoke quietly, her voice quivering. "Yeah, of course. The 'peeing' question. Of course that's why everyone's here. I'd probably ask the exact same questions if I knew that some lady touched my son's penis. I'm glad that you all are concerned parents and that you really wanted to find out what was going on." She nodded her head again as if she agreed with what the crowd demanded.

She continued, "Honestly, I was happy when I heard about this meeting. I'm into education and specifically educating little Indian kids. Obviously you all are concerned too because you have little Indian kids and understand how important it is for them to have a proper education. That's why I was happy when Mr. Elk Teeth told me about this meeting – I hoped that the 'peeing' question would be just one of many questions about your children's education. Hopefully this isn't the *only* question that you have about our class. But fair enough – thank you for this question. It's a timely question and I certainly thank you for the opportunity to answer your questions."

She stood up and pushed her chair in under the table and stepped directly in front of the crowd. She took her time and obviously felt much more confident standing up this time; although her voice was cracking and she didn't want to make eye contact when she initially introduced herself, she appeared strong now.

Ms. Jen looked directly into the wall of angry eyes on short Indian women with perms; she was ready to answer this question. "See, I was always taught, even before my professional training, that a woman and a man are only supposed to touch in certain situations. A woman, unless it's her son or nephew or other close family member, is *never* supposed to touch a boy. That's a modesty thing – I come from a modest family and that's something that my family instilled in me. Therefore, I take that very seriously. I say that to tell you that I would never, ever touch one of my students, other than to hug them, in any way unless it was absolutely necessary."

She scanned all the eyes in the room again, making sure that everybody understood that she wasn't scared. Even if it got her fired, she wanted them to understand that she believed that she was 100% right here. She was doing somebody else's job and she was going to let them know how "right" she was.

"I would *never* touch them in any sort of odd or perverted or inappropriate fashion. Heck, I wouldn't even touch them unless I thought it was absolutely necessary. Do you think that I want to get sued or fired? Here's the thing: it was necessary here. The other thing is – and I really want you to consider this carefully, because I'm not going to lie to you about it – it'll probably *still* be necessary in the future. I wish it wasn't true, but it is. See, the truth is that in my 3 years teaching here, I've taught 42 boys in kindergarten classes."

The crowd perked up and got noticeably more "on-alert" when she said that she would probably do it again in the future. They whispered to each other, "Did she just say that she would do it again??" Everybody exchanged infuriated, scandalous rez looks – the kind of look that one gives when they see a boy calling their mom's *sometimes* lover "dad" in the frozen foods section of the IGA. One lady stood up and interrupted, "42 boys?? And you're proud of that? I bet you touched every one of their penises!!"

Someone in the crowd yelled, "Prob'ly!" and the rest nodded in approval.

"No, I have not had to touch all of their penises, ma'am," Jen corrected flatly. "Thankfully, I have not had to. I have, however, touched 20 of their penises." The short, round and brown ladies in the crowd got visibly angrier when she gave the actual number. A couple of them rumbled out of the room and Jen noted that they slightly resembled little rhinoceroses as they waddled out angrily.

"Honestly, I didn't want to do it. I don't have any kids, and I honestly think it's gross to help a little boy go pee." Jen explained. "But I tried to ignore the problem my first year and a half here. After all, it wasn't my problem. It was the parents' problem, right? Why should I get my hands all stinky and nasty helping some little boy pee?"

The permed lady who'd commented that she *"prob'ly"* touched *all* of the boys' penises spoke up again. "You keep talking about a problem, lady. What the hell is the problem that you need to go molesting little boys?"

Jen looked out at the lead rhinoceros. Funny image. It kept her from getting upset and let her focus on the problem[1]. "The problem?

---

[1]*Scientific studies suggest that, at least on most Indian reservations, it is very difficult to get and/or stay mad at a rhinoceros. Scientists are still unsure as to why, they simply know that it is true. Evidently this is true of hippopotamuses as well (but scientists have a better idea of the reason for this phenomenon; evidently it goes back to the childhood game "Hungry Hungry Hippos.")*

The problem, *lady,* is that none of the boys could pee standing up. They never can when they get to my class. Never. Not one. They *always* pee sitting down. At first, I never noticed it. Why would I? I mean, I'm a woman. Of *course* everybody pees sitting down. But then I began to notice that the toilet seat was *never* up. *Never.*

"Didn't little boys leave the seat up? I know that my 29-year-old husband leaves the toilet seat up. Granted, he *is* kind of a caveman, still I *knew* that 5 and 6-year-old little boys couldn't be *that* much more evolved than my husband. Then I figured, well maybe it's too early for them to do so? Maybe they're just slow learners." Ms. Jen looked out into the crowd and, as expected, nobody agreed that their kids were slow learners.

So she moved on to the next possible theory. "But then I did a lot of research, talked to a lot of other teachers. They informed me that by 5 years old, since the vast majority of the boys in this class are 5 years old, boys should almost *invariably* pee standing up. That's what they're supposed to do! But, according to people I've spoken to, boys don't learn how to do that when there are no males present in the home. When there are no males in the household, they do not learn to pee standing up by example. Therefore, in 'single mom' situations, the mothers typically try so hard to do everything else – paying rent, cooking, cleaning – that they rarely have time to work on peeing standing up with their boys. It's simply not a priority. Plus, we don't really think about it – we're women, and why *would we* think about peeing standing up? And so the boys only see mom peeing sitting down, and it actually delays their development in education and socially."

Ms. Jen looked very confident now. She looked as if she felt she proved her point. She then decided to really take the bull by the horns and let the parents know about their accountability in this situation. "The truth is, parents, that I sent out a letter to *every single* parent informing every single one of you that 'Peeing Standing Up' was an issue. I asked for parent conferences. I got zero responses. I did the same thing the second half of last year, with my previous class. I'm a teacher – my job is to teach to the very best of my ability. If I'm not getting any response from the parents, it doesn't change my job; I still have to teach. So, I decided to integrate the issue, the problem, into the curriculum. I called it 'bathroom etiquette.' I would teach boys and girls to wash their hands, flush the toilets and wipe their bottoms. But, specifically for the past year and a half, part of my lessons has been to teach the boys who do not know how to pee standing up."

She looked into the crowd of women. "I want to respectfully ask all of you a question about how you parent at home. I honestly don't mean to pry, but I feel it would be dishonest for me not to find out; it's a very specific question, and I think that's only fair since you folks asked very specific questions about how I conduct my class. How many of you raise your boys without the boy's dad in the house?"

About three quarters of the women in the room raised their hands. She continued, "How many of you have taken time to work on peeing standing up with your boys?" None raised their hands.

"There we are," Miss Jen said. "Tell me – what can I do? Do you want me to *stop* teaching your little boys how to pee? Be honest. If you feel that it's inappropriate and that I shouldn't do it – that you'd rather take the initiative, by all means do so."

AFTERMATH

There was a lot of fallout as a result of the special community meeting. Some of the events that transpired immediately afterwards were the following:

a) Ms. Jen continued to integrate "Bathroom Etiquette" into her kindergarten curriculum with the community's support.

b) The little rhinoceros mothers formed a community group, **P**eeing **I**s **S**uper **S**ignificant (**PISS**) (the radical offshoot of the recently formed **B**oys **U**rination is **R** **P**riority or **BURP**) and embarked on a series of initiatives to make sure that local Indian boys know how to pee standing up. And wash their hands too.

c) Mr. Elk Teeth was fired because the school later discovered that he had his own peeing issues, and that was possibly/probably the reason that he was reluctant to be very vocal in this particular "peeing" controversy. Evidently, Mr. Elk Teeth had a very finicky prostate that would only allow him a satisfying discharge when he peed on his neighbor's cat; he was arrested for it one night and the school promptly let him go. The school, understandably, did not want to deal with another urination controversy.

d) Probably the most significant development that came as a result of Ms. Jen's practice was that the school, the community groups and the school board petitioned the tribal court to make sure that **"Urination Education"** was clearly written into *every* father's parenting plan with serious sanctions – 60 hours of cleaning Honeybuckets at the local pow-wow grounds after the Annual "Chili/Indian Taco Feed" – if they failed in their duties.

Everybody lived happily ever after (except the fathers who had to clean the nasty Honeybuckets). Even Mr. Elk Teeth, after he got his own cat.

Back when hip-hop was called "rap"
Back when Michael Jack was black
Before crack hit the streets
Tootie and Blair were teaching me life's facts
I had long braids and strong grades
Education was gonna be my way
Off the reservation change my situation
"I promise I'm gonna buy my mom a house someday!!"

Not that there was anything wrong with our trailer
I just thought it would be cool to not have tires on the roof.

See
Our pinto was red
Eating government cheese and reading comics
Playing freeze tag in ripped Pro Wings and Traxx
Impoverished by Reaganomics.

This was third world USA
The land that time forgot
The land that MTV forgot
To this day country music is still hot!

It's not street or urban at all
Plenty of hood drama but it's still not hood
Outhouse five hundred feet away
Our streets were rarely ever paved
Country boy representing but it's still all good.

Even when it was all bad
Those welfare years
Were the worst good times that I've ever had

Dysfunctional and broke
But
It's my home
Also
Oddly enough
The place where I discovered hip-hop.

Just like everyone else
I watched Beat Street seven million times
I was mesmerized by the Diddy Bop
I memorized all the rhymes

"Beat Street, the king of the beat
I see you rocking that beat from across the street

(uh huh)
Beat Street is a lesson too
Because you can't let the streets beat you"

The streets never beat me
But the older kids beat me
And they beat me and beat me
Into our quaint unpaved streets
See
I was doing something different
And that just wasn't too cool.

Bandanas on my arms and knees
Banana seat on my bike I'd speed
~And a~
Kick terrible rhymes in my head on the way to school

Native kid dancing in the halls
This was
Years before I discovered girls or ball
Breakdancing at pow-wows
Grass dance outfits and shawls
Jonathon Windy Boy
The nicest of us all.

I had the cheap Michael Jackson glove
Parachute pants don't help when you fall
K-Mart sweatsuit
Poplocking against the wall.

Oh yeah
Michael.
OH YEAH – MICHAEL!!

See
I feel bad for the young kids who only got to see the Michael Jackson of
his later days
The messed up looking, white-as-heck, child molester one.
That wasn't "Michael."

No
Michael WAS that cool
Michael WAS that dude
Excuse me while I digress
This isn't really part of the poem
But kids – especially boys – liked to tease that he was gay and weird
That didn't stop ANY of us from wanting to know him.

Heck naw.

I said that he was gay too
I also copied his moonwalk.

I had the fake Michael Jackson jacket
The one where the zippers didn't zip
I copied all his movements
Even the way he stuck out his bottom lip.

Mike was hip-hop.

Just like Turbo dancing with the broom was hip-hop
And
Eight of us living in a HUD house with one room was hip-hop
Jeri Curls were hip-hop

Jelly sandals during the summertime
On dusty little rez girls was hip-hop.
Doug E Fresh and Slick Rick was hip-hop
My broken down Atari Joystick was hip-hop
Jam On It *was hip-hop*
Our peanut butter and jam sandwiches with no jam on it was hip-hop
Cuz being poor was hip-hop
Going shopping all day for penny candy with quarters from the corner
store was hip-hop.

We all did that.
Metropolis to our Boondocks
New York City to the Reservation
We related to the struggle
Poor people united by music
Making the best of things and getting by.
Living for the first of the month
When we'd get flavored cereal
Get a new bandana
And think that we were fly
Until the next time mom told us to break
1-dollar food stamps for gas change
Because we had to get out to grandpa's house
There was no other way that we were gonna make it
And reminded us that we were poor.

See
Hip-hop was all of us poor people's telephone
When the ones in our homes got turned off
No ring tone
Wanted to know there were other poor people
So we didn't feel all alone
Hip-hop
Allowed us to
Talk to each through the only universal language for the young people.
Music.

VILLAGE

"Yes. Heck yes! Cripe! That *is* absolutely my business!" The large man was emphatic.

He stood up from the small dinner table, gently put his spoon down on his napkin and shook his head "yes" in exaggerated movements. His wife sat back, crossed her arms and looked up at him disgustedly as he actually put his hands over his ears, like a little kid who didn't want to hear that he couldn't have any more cake. The pouting, large man walked over in front of the petite, pretty brown woman's chair. She still had the same cold and disgusted look on her face. He leaned over her – he was very tall, probably 6'2", strongly built, with jeans and a "Journey" T-shirt on – and stretched his neck down toward the Indian woman like an osprey picking up a fish. He planted a sweet little kiss on the lady's forehead. He stood back up, furrowed his brow and got back into "emphatic" mode, "Honey, I love you very much. You know that. You are the air that I breathe and I *LOOVE* smelling the air in the morning. But, my dear lady, you fell in love with me because I speak my mind. You did not fall in love with a coward or a weenie. This is my business. If this was twenty years ago you would *want* it to be my business. Now, you want me to betray the morals and values that you fell in love with. I cannot do that. I can't pretend that these things are not my business when both of us know darn well that they're both of our business."

The beautiful older brown lady closed her eyes softly in concession. She knew that she could continue to nag him and that this argument could go on all day. It's gone on "all day" many times already; there was never really a winner. There were only opinions and perspective. Still, even though she argued, she knew in her heart of hearts that his perspective was right – she did not marry a coward. She loved his willingness to get involved when they were young and always fighting for what was right. Good God, they were fighters; didn't matter if it was IHS doctors performing forced tubal ligations or the school board not letting Indian children wear traditional regalia at their graduations. Whatever it was, *both* of them were warriors and could not help but get involved. It was in their DNA; they came from fighter blood, warrior blood.

She leaned her head back and he planted a kiss on her mouth. "I wish you weren't right, Delbert. But you are. I know you are. Still, why do *you* have to be the one who corrects everything? You're absolutely right – I didn't marry a coward. I married a strong man. Still, I wish that someone else would be the 'strong' one sometime. Why do you always have to be big brother?"

She repeated herself, however, just in case there was any doubt. "But you're right."

Still he looked reluctant as he looked out the window. It's not an argument that he wanted to "win." He wished that he did not have to get involved. But he did. Through the window he saw the two boys – probably 16 or 17 years old – walking up to the bright yellow house across the street. He wondered why the houses were always such bright colors here; it was actually a very nice house, although the front yard looked like one big parking lot. The grey Chevy Nova in the yard had pale yellow weeds growing high all the way around it; Delbert didn't recall it moving since his own son was still at home probably 18 years ago. Still, it was a nice car – he always had a thing for Novas. American muscle. The other cars in the front yard *did* work, however, and it seemed like there were always different cars there every single day. Like the dusty, maroon-colored Buick Regal that just pulled up. Who knows? It could have been a different color, but it was so dusty that he couldn't tell. The constant traffic, the lack of respect for the neighbors and the audacity to brazenly deal drugs in broad daylight all made him angry. What made him the maddest, however, was that no one other than him seemed to care.

He mumbled lowly to his wife. "They don't even try to hide what they're doing anymore, baby. That's not right. At least people used to pretend that they weren't selling drugs even if they were. We always knew who the drug dealers were, but they stayed away from our kids and didn't operate in plain sight. Now they do whatever they want to do. Now everybody around here acts scared or like they don't even care and so those young guys don't even feel like they have to hide it anymore. That's just not right, baby. I can't be one of those people who act like they don't care. I *do* care. It *is* my business, dammit." It seemed as if he were saying it as much to himself as he was to his wife.

Delbert worked himself into a pretty good rant. This was the "Hulk Hogan" moment, when the little Hulksters chanted his name and you just knew, because you've seen it a million times before, that the Hulk was about to open up a can of whoop–ass, brother. Delbert's little rant caused a vein to show up on his forehead, and his jaw to clench. Oddly, instead of grabbing the baseball bat behind the door, he grabbed his small VHS videocamera and cordless telephone off the kitchen counter; the videocamera was empty – no tapes. He walked toward the door, opened it and went outside.

He began screaming from his front porch. "My name is Delbert Big Dog and I live in this house right here. I know every single one of your families and if I see you guys take even ONE step closer to that house, I'm gonna call your parents and the police!"

The young men laughed nervously at first. He could tell they were trying to be "cool" by not getting scared. Still, the combination of the words "police," "parents" and Delbert's formidable size and volume gave them pause. They wanted to be completely dismissive, but they kept looking back at him as they walked toward the house.

Delbert stepped off his porch aggressively, taking two large and angry steps toward the yellow house. "I know you're over there buying that crap. I've seen you getting those damn oxycontin pills and I've recorded you purchasing and I've recorded the idiots inside selling that poison to you!" He raised the camera up in the air and kept walking toward the boys.

The boys stopped dead in their tracks before they reached the yellow house's front porch. "Don't worry, I've already called the FBI on them and they're watching that house!! Matter of fact, you don't even have to take a step closer – I see your license plates. I'm calling them right now unless you get out of here right this second!" He started dialing on his cordless phone. The two boys ran back out to their dusty Buick Regal and sped away.

Delbert walked slowly back into his house. He wondered when those boys would be back. He wondered if any of them would ever come to his house to test out if he was really ready to do something if push came to shove. He hoped, desperately, that one of them would someday.

"Baby, when we were kids, you know that this would have never happened. It seems like when we were growing up, people were always too nosy. You just couldn't do anything like what they're doing across the street, baby. I remember one time, I got into a fight at Indian Days and our fight broke out somebody's camper window. The guy was tough as rip and he slammed me up against the truck. I don't even remember if I won or if he won, alls I remember is that I hurt for days afterwards and that we dented that truck up good. When I got home, I was in trouble because my dad thought I got beat up, but also because we beat up that poor old guy's truck. They found out in the 15 minutes that it took me to get home! And heck, that was before anybody had phones! People were always so nosy!"

He looked at his wife. "Now, *nobody's* nosey even though *everybody* notices! It's just that now nobody wants to say anything. Everybody closes their curtains and turns off their lights when something 'bad' happens. Nobody wants the police to ask them any questions. Nobody wants to admit that they ever see anything. They're cowards."

He looked sad, wistful, and nostalgic. He remembered when this reservation was very, very poor; that was only about 15 years ago. Back then, the time that he calls "B.C." for "Before Casino," everybody knew each other in this town. Kids played in the streets, there were cookouts during the summertime. During the winter time, there were snowball fights and kids "hooking cars." In the time "B.C.," it wasn't always good – being poor wasn't fun most of the time. But back then the community was a community, not just a bunch of people who happened to be living next to each other.

In recent times, however, since the Tribe got money from their casino, a whole bunch of new folks moved there. The new folks were mainly raised in cities away from the reservation. Delbert wasn't crazy about all the newcomers; it wasn't because they always thought that they knew better and that their ideas would "save us." No, he'd been dealing with white people his whole life, so he was used to people like that; that wasn't what bothered him the most. It was that they wanted to live here, in "simplicity," soak up the resources and jobs that the casino created, but not contribute anything at all to this reservation.

He thought, "Yeah, they're tribal members, I suppose...but they never grew up here. Obviously they did not want to be here before. They only moved here after the money got here and the jobs got here. They never endured a hard day of life here on the reservation – they don't remember what it was like when our only chance to survive was to rely on each other." Now, instead of cookouts, neighborhood fights, stick games and play between neighbor kids and sleepovers, there's closed curtains and high fences. There're neighbors that he didn't know. There're cars that drive by without waving. There are people who don't take the time to speak to the winos selling stuff at the grocery store. They treat the winos like they're unwanted. Delbert thought, "Those winos have more right to be here than those newcomers do."

But the biggest problem is that, since the newcomers came, there was a pronounced lack of involvement in the neighborhood kids' lives. He muttered to his wife, "Everybody plumb doesn't want to get involved. It's sad. There are no more 'Leftys.'"

Delbert remembered, literally around the corner from where he lived now, the day that Lefty brutally spanked him. It was a warm fall day and all the boys in the housing area that he grew up in were having a "shingle fight." "Shingle fights" happened from time to time in the fall when the tribe's housing department had excess money that it had to spend by the end of the year.

Many times those housing departments would go out and replace the roofing shingles on elders' houses, which left big piles of shingles on the sides of the houses. The boys would go and haul the shingles away and make teams to have huge shingle battles. Ninjas were the big thing when Delbert was a kid; it seemed like everyone wanted to be a ninja. Since there were no karate classes or other martial arts on this reservation, this was the boys' one chance to be ninja-like. They threw the shingles like Chinese stars and kicked around and made lots of noise. It was a lot of fun. Sometimes too much fun.

Delbert smiled as he leaned on the kitchen counter. The time Lefty had to whip him was "too much fun."

LEFTY

That fateful day, the boys fought each other viciously. Delbert's team, the "Snake Eyes," was destroying the other team, the "Storm Shadows." The boys sometimes cut each other and sometimes bruised each other a little bit. Still, it was nothing they couldn't handle. Plus, the truth was that everything was fine because 1) ultimately the shingles really could do just a *little* bit of damage, but were not inherently dangerous, and also 2) boys just get hurt sometimes. It just happens; they're supposed to. So, people never complained about the boys hurting each other en masse once a year because it wouldn't happen for another year. This time, something went awry and grown-ups noticed.

In the midst of a sustained flurry of shingle fire from the Snake Eyes, one of the elders, whose roof was getting redone, came outside. Typically the protocol among the boys was to stop immediately when a grown-up walked in the vicinity or drove by. Unfortunately, this time – happy to keep the Storm Shadows firmly off-balance and losing – Delbert kept throwing, like Fernando Valenzuela, as the elder walked out to her Dodge Aspen. The boys on the Storm Shadow team appropriately were shocked at Delbert's behavior and were ducking everyplace that they could. One of them had to jump behind the Aspen to avoid Delbert's madman-like throwing. Then – in an act that *had* to be temporary insanity – Delbert actually gave chase to the kid who ducked behind the Aspen and the elder and it looked like he threw a shingle *toward* the elder.

Accounts differ on what happened. Some say that he actually he threw *at* the elder for being "in the way." Some say that it was just bad aim with an unfortunate result. Either way, the shingle bounced off the elder's neck and left a welt there. It was nothing permanent or even serious. Still, it was something that should not have happened.

The other boys went silent – the laughter stopped. Delbert swears, to this day, that a tumbleweed blew across the street. He also claims that a solar eclipse occurred simultaneously and that the sky went dark. As the shingle fell to the ground from the elder's neck, a big, brown, sweaty Indian man – working in the September sun – walked over toward the group of boys. The big Indian man wore a red bandana on his head, jean shorts rolled up at the bottom and had a big chew in his bottom lip. That man was Lefty. Lefty was one of the men reroofing the elders' houses and had been working all day stepping in tar and nailing shingles into the roof in the hot sun. Still, when he saw Delbert hit the elder with the shingle, Lefty made it his business to put his hammer down, come down from the roof of the house and literally put Delbert over his knee and start spanking him. Hard. Many times. No one said a word.

Now, Lefty wasn't his dad. Lefty wasn't his uncle. Lefty wasn't even a close neighbor or friend of the family. Yet, Lefty *was* a man who lived in this Indian community and knew that little Indian kids disrespecting older Indian people was not a good thing. It wasn't an acceptable thing. It was not something that he could excuse – in fact, it was something that he *had* to do something about. It was his business.

See, Lefty was invested in *his* community. He felt like it was his community; that was the difference between him and the newcomers to this reservation. It wasn't that they were new or that they drank lattes instead of real coffee. The reason that Delbert didn't like them was because they did not see this reservation as "their" community. Those newcomers had no sense of ownership like Delbert had, like Lefty had; the whole reservation could go to hell in a handbasket for all they cared, as long as they had their job (where they never had to go to work on Friday) and the cost of living was less than in the city.

Delbert was different. He cared.

He came from a long line of people who cared and who made getting involved their business. Just like Lefty did. Lefty taught Delbert that it takes a whole village to raise children. He taught him that if he were going to care for the reservation, he would have to care for all of it, the good and the bad. Lefty taught Delbert to make everything his business, because everything that happens on the reservation will eventually affect him. He taught him not to be there because of a per capita check or a job or because the reservation "cleaned up." Instead, he should love this place – warts and all.

Lefty taught Delbert that little Indian boys who were bad enough to disrespect old Indian folks with no consequences would grow up to be criminals. He understood why Lefty spanked him mercilessly all those years earlier; Lefty didn't want any criminals to grow up and rob him or his family. He was smart to start the prevention then. In that way, Delbert's shingle throwing mishap was absolutely Lefty's business.

Now, when Delbert saw nonsense like these drug dealings going on across the street, he couldn't lie and say that it wasn't his business. It would be so much easier to act like all the newcomers and just work on his yard. But he couldn't. He loved this place. He loved his people. He wanted better for his people. He leaned over the kitchen counter and gave thanks for Lefty's painful lesson; he taught him that everything that happened here was "absolutely" his business.

SPECIAL

The mean girls told her
"Stop acting like you're Indian!"

She was too thin
To be in
Plus
Her jeans were too fancy.

Daddy moved from the rez at age six
Made money in technology
Then entered politics.
Married an Indian military brat bride
Who never had to use Nix
Never ate beef stew
Nor drank powdered milk
Parents moved away
"Things are too rough there."
Lived every day with the guilt.
So
They moved back
To
Raise their kids at home.

She was special.
Like trust funds and per capita payments
Used to pay college tuition.
Teachers paid her extra attention
She got straight A's
Daddy's military discipline
Much bigger motivator than detention.

The mean girls made fun of her

"American Indian Barbie"
Perfectly painted nails
On both her fingers and toes
They told her "Go back home
Your family will never really know

What it feels like to be a real Indian."

"You're Indian in blood only
You've never been poor."

She said "I am home.
I have no place else to go."
Stopped raising her now-unpainted hand in class
Now
Sometimes she doesn't even go.

She didn't want to be special.

The mean boys told him
"Stop acting like you're Indian!"

He tried again
Still
He didn't fit in

They didn't like his talk.
"Indians don't speak with a lisp
Barely above a whisper
Plus
You switch when you walk."
Blood was undeniable
Still
They said that Indian guys don't do that
Whatever "that" was that wasn't cool at the time.

He was special.

Like the rainbow that showed

After Noah's great storm
A promise that God loves us all
Loves even the delicate little men
Found beaten in the high school hall.
After school
Kids are cruel
Slumped against the locker wall.

He just wanted to be friends
He thought that they were his friends too
Wouldn't tell the principal who they were.

The delicate Indian boy tried hard to suppress "it"
Toned down the way he dressed
Teased other delicate boys and suggested
They were the ones who were different.
It surely wasn't him.

He didn't want to be special.

The mean girls told her
"Stop acting like you're Indian!"

Pale skin didn't fit in
Beauty brought too much attention
Sparkly eyes could not remain anonymous
Underlying constant source of tension
Outstanding
Not typical
Demanding
Comment from folks who didn't quite feel as noticed.

She was special.
Like a supermoon
She appeared closer to
What they wanted to be
Since they simply could not be
They would not acknowledge
That she was special.

Extraordinary features
Still
Such a vulnerable creature
Because
Everybody wants to fit in.
Even those who are special.

Anger, profanity and alcohol
Great equalizers
"Maybe if I act just like them
Nobody will be the wiser
Think that I am 'acting' Indian

Maybe then I'll just be."

Sometimes it sucks to be special.

ABOUT DKMAI

Don't Know Much About Indians (but i wrote a book about us anyways) ("DKMAI") was initially Gyasi's attempt to create some modern mythology and/or archetypes for Native people. He was heavily inspired by the "Napi" stories[1] that his maternal grandpa Percy Bullchild both told and wrote about. He was also inspired by the big book of Greek mythology that the family always had on their old, warped coffee table. Finally, when he was in 5th grade, in Mr. Higgins' class at Napi Elementary, Mr. Higgins assigned the class to read The Brothers Grimm. All of those sources – Napi stories, Greek mythology, and the Brothers Grimm stories – utilized morality tales and oftentimes simplified characters in order to teach valuable lessons. DKMAI is Gyasi's attempt to replicate that structure and those lessons without the very clear lesson at the end.

Of course, the title is somewhat tongue-in-cheek; Gyasi knows plenty about Indians. In fact, he's been Indian pretty much all of his life, and lived on no less than 4 reservations. Still, Gyasi doesn't "know" Indians the way his grandpa did – like many Natives nowadays, he's a product of pan-Indianism[2], urban Indian survival instincts, Ivy League schools, Saturday Night Live, MTV, hip-hop music, etc. His grandpa lived mainly amongst Natives his entire life; Gyasi walks almost every day primarily among non-Natives, even on the reservations. Demographics have changed, circumstances have changed.

Therefore, DKMAI is about many of those experiences, both on-reservation and off-reservation. There are experiences in DKMAI that every single Native person will be able to relate to; there are others that are Gyasi's alone. Still, there is enough commonality in DKMAI that Natives and non-Natives alike will be able to learn about some of the very unique challenges, victories, tensions, and heartbreaks that Native people face. This book will teach you, regardless of your ethnicity, religion, tribe, or worldview. Some of the lessons in DKMAI are heartbreaking; some are beautiful. Many times, as oftentimes happened in Napi tales, Greek mythology and Brothers Grimm stories, contemporary Native stories are both heartbreaking and beautiful at the same time. DKMAI captures that.

[1] For more information, please go to http://blackfootdigitallibrary.org/en/category/subject-lcsh/napi

[2] I think that this PDF article has a pretty good explanation of "pan-Indianism." Read it – the person who wrote that is smarter than I am. Still, to me, pan-Indianism is a very pragmatic blending of various Native cultures, biology (intermarrying) and practices to give one a sense of community in very decidedly non-Native locales. Still, read this: https://journals.ku.edu/index.php/amerstud/article/view/2223/2182